Mission Accomplished

The very best of Duffel Blog, Volume One

By Paul Szoldra, and the contributing writers of Duffel Blog

Duffel Media LLC
2370 S. El Camino Real, Suite 220
San Clemente, CA 92672

Disclaimer: Duffel Blog is in no way, shape, or form, a real news outlet. Unless otherwise noted, all content on Duffel Blog's website and in this book, is satirical, as Duffel Blog represents a parody of a news organization. No composition should be regarded as truthful, and no reference of an individual, company, or military unit seeks to inflict malice or emotional harm.

All characters, groups, and military units appearing in these works are fictitious. Any resemblance to real persons, living or dead, or actual military units and companies is purely coincidental.

For Ron

We miss you. Thank you for keeping us laughing.

And as always, thank you for your service.

This page intentionally left blank.

This page intentionally left blank.

This page intentionally left blank.

Ok, this joke is getting old. We promise that's the last one.

This page intentionally left blank.

Table of Contents

Foreword

I'll never forget the time that Duffel Blog published an article saying that I was actually Sgt. Maj. Carlton Kent.

I can't forget, because to this day I get emails from duped souls who think I'm actually the 16th Sergeant Major of the Marine Corps — 5 years later.

With the rise of social media within the military community, otherwise voiceless service members were given an outlet to openly criticize and engage in vocal free thought like never before. Few outlets have encapsulated and embraced this as well as Duffel Blog.

Behind the biting wit and outrageous headlines is a satirical prowess that not only engages the reader with pointed absurdist humor, but does so with the intent to challenge every level of the military experience.

The impact of Duffel Blog cannot be understated, as it has become a colloquial norm at this point within the military community to verify that any ridiculous headline didn't originate from www.duffelblog.com

It has happened to the best of us.

This is the magic of Duffel Blog: Able to say anything about anyone, and with never a shortage of people in the Facebook comments who just haven't figured it out yet.

On top of all of that, I am honored to be able to call Paul a close friend. Frequently entertaining my insane ideas in late night exchanges, even though I typically ignore his advice at every turn.

It is because of his perseverance and his commitment to the impartial ideal that the body of works he has assembled, with his crack team of military insider writers, will stand the test of time when other military-centric brands die off into obscurity.

I think I speak for everyone when I say I look forward to many more years of Duffel Blog to come.

Maximilian *"Do Your Leading Marines MCI"* Uriarte
Creator of Terminal Lance

Introduction

In the spring of 2012, I started a blog on a website I built to help transitioning veterans find the right college after service. That website never really gained traction, but the blog, which I named Duffel Blog, certainly did.

Duffel Blog launched under the banner of now-defunct CollegeVeteran.com on March 4, 2012. The first article ever published, "Tired Of 'Chair Force' Nickname, Air Force Colonel Bans Chairs," was initially read by perhaps a dozen or so people.

Now as I write this nearly five years later, a typical Duffel Blog article may be read by tens of thousands of people, and sometimes millions. The small, niche website where every article was once written by just me now boasts more than 100 contributing writers from every branch of service.

The growth and support of Duffel Blog from members of the military and veteran community is something I never could have imagined.

Over the years, Duffel Blog has entertained the US military with articles on a broad range of topics, skewering everything from reflective belts, PowerPoint briefings, and junior lieutenants, to top generals, military strategy, and the President of the United States.

Before Duffel Blog, a military service member may have complained about an idiotic policy to the person standing next to them in formation. Now, a service member writing on Duffel Blog can use humor as a weapon and reach millions, to include the top leadership of the US military, such as Chairman of the Joint Chiefs Gen. Joseph Dunford and Secretary of Defense Jim Mattis — both of whom are fans of the site.

It has been an absolute honor and privilege to see this website grow in both size and impact, and though there have been many factors that have contributed to its success, Duffel Blog owes its rise to fans like you.

I'd like to sincerely thank you for purchasing this book.

As long as there are people like you reading and supporting our work, Duffel Blog will continue to serve the US military for many years to come. Thank you so much for being a fan.

And thank you for your service.

Paul Szoldra
Founder and Editor-in-Chief of Duffel Blog

How this book is structured

This book is a collection of 100 of the best articles ever published to Duffel Blog. The choice was not easy: In five years of existence, we've published more than 2,000 articles.

Like you would find on the Duffel Blog website, most articles in this book include an article's headline, image, and content. But for the purposes of this book, and for the benefit of fans, on select articles we have included more — a back story, great impact, or some other 'insider' knowledge of a story that most people have never heard before.

These sections are titled "Behind the Blog," and they are written solely by our founder, Paul Szoldra.

Tired Of 'Chair Force' Nickname, Air Force Colonel Bans Chairs

By Paul Sharpe

TAMPA, Fla. — The Commander of the 6th Air Mobility Wing at MacDill Air Force Base announced today that he would no longer allow chairs to be used by his airmen. In his weekly command-wide email, Col. Lenny Richoux stressed the importance of good posture, physical fitness, and "standing tall."

"We must remember that chairs are detrimental to good posture, mobility, and discipline," he wrote. "So, effective immediately, all chairs are to be removed from offices."

Derrick Crowley, the command chief master sergeant, wasn't buying it.

"This isn't about posture. The Colonel's just plain sick and tired of this 'Chair Force' moniker. Being around all these CENTCOM door-kickers all day long means we have to put up with all their crap."

Richoux denied that this had anything to do with the "unofficial Air Force nickname."

"Our Airmen, whether they are flying jets, piloting UAV's, or gathering intelligence, are always sitting down. This stuff has got to be bad for their back," he said.

Some airmen at the command were angered.

"How the hell am I supposed to work under these conditions?" asked Senior Airman Gregory Jones. "So, we use chairs. Big deal. It doesn't mean we all should be at standing desks like a bunch of idiot hippies."

Many chairs on the base have already been removed in order to meet the deadline of March 9. Richoux closed his email with a sharp warning.

"Anyone caught sitting down will be court martialed. Don't be the one."

BEHIND THE BLOG

This was the first story we ever published on Duffel Blog, which was then The Duffel Blog (we later dropped "the" from the name after a meeting with Sean Parker).

I didn't really know what kind of impact this story would have, or if anyone would ever read it, but I do remember being somewhat afraid of using real names. At the time, I had no idea what kind of First Amendment protections there were regarding satire. I used the real names of the colonel and sergeant major at the command, but in the back of mind, I legitimately thought people from MacDill Air Force Base were going to come knocking on my door and take me away.

I guess they didn't want to leave their chairs.

Captain Charged With Manslaughter After Leaving Lieutenant Unattended In Parked Car

By Sgt B

FORT HUACHUCA, Ariz. — The company commander of a signal unit was arrested on manslaughter charges after leaving his executive officer unattended in a parked car Friday, military police confirmed.

Capt. Rick Halset, 30, was apprehended after his executive officer, Lt. Carl Higgs, 26, was found dead, still locked inside the vehicle.

Higgs was apparently left in the car outside the post exchange while Halset went inside to grab a few things.

"I told him I'd be right back, I didn't think I needed to leave the car running. I really only meant to be gone a minute," said an obviously distraught Halset.

Bystanders reported the lieutenant had locked himself in the car with the windows up in the blistering Arizona sun. By the time Halset had returned, Higgs had suffered a heat stroke and passed away before base medics could respond.

Carolyn Tyler, an army spouse, was heading to the PX when she spotted Higgs in the car.

"I was walking in to get some Boone's Farm for me and the hubby to enjoy when he got back from the field and I saw this poor lieutenant stuck in that car," Tyler said. "It's over 100 degrees here. What kind of monster would leave that little guy in a hot car with the windows up?"

Others tried to assist the young officer in unlocking the doors so he could get to safety.

"I tried to coax him towards the door so maybe he'd hit the button, but I couldn't get him to listen to me," said Spc. Byron Tiller. "I've seen people do cruel stuff like that to lieutenants before, and it's just not right. Unfortunately, we got there too late to make much of a difference and before I called for a medic he was already headed out."

"I just couldn't bring myself to tell the captain what happened to the lieutenant," 1st Sgt. Bryan McGraw told reporters. "He didn't seem to understand why he wasn't moving anymore, so I just told him Higgs had to go to a B-billet in recruiting where he was going to be very happy. I even promised him we'd go to Fort Benning, or hell, even West Point, and pick him out a new lieutenant. But he just kept crying 'I don't want a new lieutenant, I want Higgs!'"

"I really feel bad for the young captain," he added.

The incident has forced the Army to review its policies on the humane treatment of lieutenants.

"Some people think getting a lieutenant is as easy as feeding them, but there are a lot of other things, like training, mentorship, etcetera," said Col. Steven Chang, Halset and Higgs' battalion commander. "And when you get these irresponsible CO's who get lieutenants and then neglect them, that's how you get these dangerous lieutenants who are just going to get fired and end up in some staff section with nobody who loves them, waiting on a mentor who's probably never going to show up. That's why I always adopt my staff from the S-3 or company office."

Even enlisted soldiers are rallying to help young lieutenants with the formation of the ASPCA, or Army Specialists, Privates, and Corporals Association. The ASPCA has a mission of "mentoring and caring for lieutenants until they survive to make captain," according to ASPCA spokesperson Spc. Gina Woods.

While the Provost Marshall's office at Fort Huachua is seeking to charge Halset with manslaughter, Col. Chang has succeeded in reducing the charge to one misdemeanor count of neglect of a junior officer.

"I listened to Col. Chang's argument, and I realized that it's not really that young captain's fault," said Maj. Stephanie Cook. "That's a lot of responsibility to place on a young officer, and we're proud that he remembered to feed him and take him for runs everyday."

Hero MP Stops Speeding Car Going 8 Mph, Saves Countless Lives

By Ron

STUTTGART, GERMANY — Local military police officer William Moya is being called "an all-American hero" by his command today after his actions were credited with saving countless lives on the base.

During a recent speed-enforcement activity, Moya, a 28-year old staff sergeant, pulled over a motorist who was blazing through the Patch Barracks Shoppette parking lot with a "callous disregard for the safety of other personnel."

Since Patch Barracks is in Europe, it uses the metric system. The speed limit in front of the Shoppette is 10 km per hour, or approximately 6 mph.

"When we saw that car careening through the Shoppette parking lot, we couldn't believe it at first," said Sgt. 1st Class Tommy Trejo, a veteran MP and Moya's supervisor. "I said to myself, 'This guy is gonna get someone killed.'"

Moya spotted the car hurtling toward him and sprang into action. He took a sip of his coffee, set it on the ground, picked up his radar gun, turned it on, and pointed it straight at the furiously accelerating death machine.

The gun's verdict? Guilty.

"I was just really surprised to tell you the truth," said Moya. "We're not playing Need for Speed here."

The fearless Moya then surprised everyone by stepping in front of the driver and signaling him to stop.

"It was like a scene out of a movie," Trejo said. "With no regard for his own safety, Moya walked straight in front of that crazy asshole. If that guy wouldn't have stopped, [Moya] would have only had 10 seconds to jump back onto the sidewalk, 15 seconds tops."

Luckily, the driver, whose name MPs are not releasing out of fear of public reprisal, did stop. Moya initially cited him for speeding and reckless endangerment.

During the traffic stop, Moya noticed the driver was wearing his physical fitness uniform without a reflective belt. The lack of reflective belt was not a violation since the driver was inside his vehicle, so the quick-thinking Moya asked him to step outside. When the driver obeyed, Moya was then able to cite him for the uniform violation.

"Staff Sgt. Moya is a credit to the force," said Capt. James Burr, his company commander. "We believe that the more violations we catch, the safer our community is. Moya's ability to turn one violation into two or sometimes three is a testament to how safe he is keeping everyone."

Despite the praise of his supervisors, Moya remains humble.

"I was just doing my job," Moya said. "The real heroes here are the people who decided that the speed limit should be 6 miles an hour. They're the ones we should all be thanking."

AWOL Private Returns After Seven Years With Box Of Grid Squares

By Sgt B

FORT BRAGG, N.C. — Army Pvt. Steven Gerner disappeared seven years ago, officially listed as AWOL. His family, friends and Army buddies all assumed he'd had an accident or lost his nerve and no one ever expected to see him again. He returned yesterday, only to find himself arrested by Military Police. What happened in between is a tale too implausible to be disbelieved.

Gerner joined the Army in 2004 out of Sangre de Cristo, Arizona. He reached his first assignment of infantry in 2005, eager to please, and wanting to belong.

"Well, it was my first day, and I guess I was pretty nervous and not really sure of what to do," said Gerner. "Before I had even reported in to the first sergeant, a sergeant, and two specialists walked up to me. Of course, I did what I was trained to do, and immediately snapped to the position of parade rest and gave them all the greeting of the day."

He continued: "After that, they started laughing and talking among themselves about 'this gay-ass slick-sleeve saying good morning,' whoever that was. Before I knew it, the sergeant was in my face and told me to find a box of grid squares. I tried to explain I didn't know where to find that! Hell, I didn't even know where the unit supply office was, but he didn't relent."

Soldiers new to units often become subject to pranks that are as old as the Army itself. Often, these pranks involve seasoned soldiers sending the new private on a quest for objects that don't exist. Chemlight batteries, exhaust samples, frequency grease, and muzzle blast have been sought after by well-intended, yet unaware, junior soldiers.

Former Sgt. Zachary Willburn, who sent Gerner to find the box of grid squares, took a break from "smoking flavored tobacco" to speak with Duffel Blog by phone from his home in Boulder, Colorado.

"Yeah, Gerner. That guy went AWOL his first day after I told him to get some grid squares. I've never seen someone take off so fast. Me and the other guys had a pretty big laugh, but, uh, we kinda expected him to come back a few minutes later. I never saw him again after that," said Willburn. "After a few days, they officially marked him as AWOL. We all thought he deserted because we were heading to Iraq in a month."

Gerner claims to have found the elusive box of grid squares in a remote region in the Himalayan Mountains.

"At first, I spent about a year traveling across the United States, Canada, and then South America. After I couldn't find it in Colombia, I almost gave up hope — you can find anything in Colombia. That's when I caught a flight to the Middle East. I figured, it's the cradle of civilization; if this exists, it has to be there."

When asked how he was able to afford the airline tickets, Gerner explained: "Apparently when they marked me AWOL they never stopped my pay, so I just used what I had at the time to move around. I also got tax free pay and combat pay while my unit was in Iraq for 18 months. I filled out travel vouchers through the Defense Travel System over the course of the last seven years, but I still haven't seen any of that money."

While he ultimately found the mystical box, Gerner related some dark times during his journey.

"Once, I was making my way across Iraq and ran into a pretty crazy firefight. The other soldiers were screaming at me, telling me to 'get inside the wire,' whatever that means, but I told them I had to go find a box of grid-squares or my sergeant was going to kill me. They all started laughing until some stuff started falling out of the sky and blowing up, I think they might have been the air-launched improvised explosive devices that I heard about at Basic Training."

Gerner's quest had a happy ending, after one final twist.

The official report released from his unit states that he returned to his unit Friday morning with an odd-shaped box, after being marked AWOL seven years ago to the day. The current company commander, Capt. Gregory Schwarz, was stunned.

"Pvt. Gerner was arrested for desertion, but the interviewing JAG officer released him as soon as he heard his story. He won't be receiving non-judicial punishment, or a court-martial for being AWOL, as it has been found he was simply following orders. Truthfully, he was officially separated from the Army after his six-year contract was up."

Schwarz elaborated: "In light of his actions, a review board has found in his favor and will be upgrading his dishonorable discharge to an honorable discharge. He has also been awarded the Iraq campaign medal with two stars, the Global War on Terrorism Expeditionary medal, and the Afghanistan Campaign medal with one star, as we found in our investigation he traveled through all of these areas while looking for this box."

"Gerner was also awarded four Army Commendation Medals due to his unit being deployed four times during his 7-year journey," he added.

Gerner's mother was ecstatic at the news of her son's return.

"I'm so proud of my baby boy. We were so worried while he was gone. I guess I've always kind of known my son was destined for great things, ever since that large black recruiter with the sunglasses on told me when he was just a child, 'he's the one.' I didn't know what he meant at the time, but now it's all so clear."
His recruiter, Sgt. 1st Class Philip Stokes, recounted his meeting with the then-18-year-old shortly before he signed his papers, sealing his fate.

"He asked me about Iraq. I said, 'unfortunately, no one can be told what Iraq is. You have to see it for yourself.'"

Even though his journey was harrowing at times, Gerner expresses nothing but fond memories of his time in the Army, especially when he searched in Tahiti for three years.

BEHIND THE BLOG

This epic tale was written by Sgt B, one of the first (of what would later become many) contributors to join the site. B wrote me an email on March 22, 2012 with a brief intro and a writing sample, which fortunately, made me laugh. That was basically the only standard I had for potential writers at that point.

I wrote B a couple of days later to tell him it'd be awesome if he wrote for the site. "Now, let's talk about pay and benefits," I told him. "Pay is going to be somewhere around zero, but benefits are that you can have the joy of making people laugh (and laughing at people who think the story is real in the comments section)."

While the laughing benefit is still in effect, I now also pay writers for each article published, ever since they caught wind of the advertising banners on the site.

Army Study Finds Marines' Tun Tavern Was Actually A Gay Bar

By Jack Mandaville

PHILADELPHIA, Penn. – A recent archaeological study commissioned and funded by the United States Army has yielded a surprising discovery just east of Front Street in Philadelphia, Pennsylvania. Some military historians are calling this the most astonishing military-themed find since the unearthing of the Terracotta Army in rural China.

The dig has uncovered evidence suggesting that Tun Tavern — the beloved institutional Mecca of the United States Marine Corps — was an active gay bar when the Corps' first officers used it to recruit the original Continental Marines in 1775.

"This find has confirmed what many of us suspected for years," said the study's NCOIC, Army Sgt. 1st Class Craig Mangas. "It's apparent, regarding the nature of current Marines, that they've evolved from some sort of ultra-queer genome."

The original Tun Tavern burned down in 1781 and the space is now shared with Interstate-95 where it passes along Penn's Landing. The initial goal of the dig was to locate any physical clues that could tie modern Marines with the past.

Mangas told Duffel Blog about the origins of the study.

"Many of the Army personnel who were stationed with Marines in Iraq and Afghanistan noticed a lot of primordial homo-erotic tendencies within their lower enlisted ranks," he said. "The way they would casually smack each other's asses, their brazen displays of nudity amongst their comrades, it was incredible to see. Plus, there was that time I saw two dudes going down on each other behind a port-o-shitter on Camp Leatherneck. That was pretty fuckin' gay."

"We became obsessed with tracking down the root cause of this behavior," he added. "So we decided the best thing to do was dig up their ancestral homeland."

The dig, which started in early May, saw little progress until recently when archaeologists stumbled upon the tavern's outhouse in the cellar.

"That was some of the gayest shit I've ever seen," said Dr. J. Becifius Vanderford of Penn College, an archaeologist on the dig. "We feel like we've unlocked a historical treasure-trove of gaydom that will help the modern Marine Corps better understand who they are."

The site has not been opened to the media yet, but members of the excavation team have given us some details about their discovery.

"We found walls that had 'WAGNER COVETS THY PHALLUS' written all over them," said Spc. Nathan Bules of Tuscaloosa, Ala., a soldier who was on the dig as part of a mandatory working party assignment. "Somebody even carved 'SEMPER SEMEN' near an old dartboard. I mean, that daggone nonsense was everywhere. We also saw a bunch of pewter martini glasses everywhere and it seemed like you couldn't move five feet without stepping on a doody-laced, wood-carved dildo. It's like these guys were in some sort of gaymosexual heat."

Perhaps the most noteworthy find was a decaying book pulled from behind the bar.

"The book had the owner listed as Josiah Wagner," Bules told us. "It's pretty clear that he was the ringleader of the entire orgy. But the most astonishing part was the fact that the records showed the bar was listed as 'Fun Tavern.' It appears there was a misprint sometime ago and the 'Tun' part stuck. This guy knew exactly what he was doing by naming it that."

Dr. Vanderford offered his hypothesis on why the location was chosen as the Marines' first recruiting center.

"It would make a lot of sense that Maj. Samuel Nicholas chose that spot because of the tremendous amount of men willing to do anything for a good time," he said. "Once the 18-wheeler arrives to haul off these dildos, we'll be able to get a better understanding of this site."

"It's more than just a great historical find," added Mangas. "It gives an entirely new meaning to being in the 'City of Brotherly Love.'"

IED Emplacement Postponed For Another Goddamned Safety Brief

By G-Had

TREKH NAWA, AFGHANISTAN — The planned emplacement of an improvised explosive device on Main Service Road Tulley was delayed again, according to local Taliban leader Mullah Ahmidullah, because all the emplacers had to attend "another goddamned safety brief."

"We were all set to go this morning, until I got my turban chewed by Mullah Hayatullah," Ahmidullah complained.

According to Ahmidullah, four of his emplacers still had to undergo Operational Risk Management, Motorcycle Safety, and Gender Sensitivity Training.

"Seriously?" Mullah Ahmidullah exclaimed. "Gender Sensitivity Training? The last woman we saw was the one we stoned to death for smiling!"

Mullah Ahmidullah runs a cell of Taliban fighters that emplaces IEDs on the local roads, targeting American convoys and Afghan police vehicles. At least that was before the Quetta Shurah put a new emphasis on safety and risk management in the field.

In the last two weeks, Mullah Ahmidullah's cell has only managed to emplace two IEDs, a decline which he primarily attributes to a now "endless" series of classes his fighters have to attend.

"Tuesday is 'Music is the Devil,' Wednesday is 'Drugs: How to Grow and Sell Them,' and Thursday is 'Don't Kill Yourself Until We Get the Vest Strapped On.'"

According to Mullah Mubarak in Herat Province, the new focus on safety briefs is impacting other Taliban units as well.

"Just last week I had one of my best executioners pulled because his swim qualification wasn't up-to-date! How are we supposed to properly cut infidels' throats on our next propaganda film without him?"

Taliban Shadow Governor Mullah Hayatullah, reached at his home in Quetta, Pakistan, confirmed the new emphasis on safety. He also said that the change is being driven largely by what he referred to as "recent stories in the media."

Earlier this year, the Khaaba Press alleged that two Taliban fighters in Kunduz Province were caught flying a kite. Shortly after that, a Taliban cameraman in Helmand Province was beheaded for forgetting to praise Allah while filming a suicide bombing. The final straw, however, may have come last week when the Haqqani Network discovered that their unit logo was actually a Danish cartoon of the Prophet Muhammad.

Others blame a public outcry by Mothers of Afghanistan over unnecessary Taliban fatalities caused by poor safety, such as the infamous YouTube video of four Taliban killed while attempting to strap a 300-pound IED to a donkey. In response, Taliban Supreme Leader Mullah Omar promised a renewed emphasis on "keeping our boys safe."

Mullah Hayatullah said that the Quetta Shurah understands the frustration some may have, but added "that's why we get paid the big Afghanis."

"Mullah Omar feels that we need to be focusing on the 'whole Taliban' concept, instead of this narrow focus on combat operations in Afghanistan," he said.

"We need to be thinking of where we want to be ten years down the road, and getting back to our roots as an anti-Israel force in readiness. After all, Afghanistan doesn't have a Taliban because it needs one. It has a Taliban because it wants one!"

Veteran Decides To Start Running Again, Next Thursday Morning

By Armydave

PORTLAND, Ore. — Earlier today, local Army veteran Thomas Swanson made the mental decision to pick up running again, but not today. He will likely begin next Thursday morning, or maybe Saturday, depending on how early he wakes up.

"I've really gotten out of shape, man," said Swanson, a former paratrooper who used to sometimes run six miles a day.

Swanson, a now-275 lb overweight man proud to be a former member of the 82nd Airborne who once had washboard abs, spoke with reporters from his mother's basement while surrounded by exercise equipment only used by physically-fit spiders.

"I mean, I constantly tell people how I used to be able to do these many push-ups or that many sit-ups," he said, while shoving spoonful's of caramel ice cream into his mouth.

Swanson spent four years on active-duty where he routinely performed physical training up to five times a week. At peak fitness, he was capable of running two miles in 11 minutes and 23 seconds, doing 106 push-ups in two minutes, and 84 sit-ups.

Now, he walks approximately 45 extra steps at work in order to take the elevator rather than ride the escalator.

"He really let himself go," said Kimberly Brookings, Swanson's long-time girlfriend. "When I met him, he had just gotten out of the Army. Sure, he wasn't ripped or anything, but he was generally a fit guy."

Sources confirm that Swanson recently purchased a new pair of running shoes from the local mall. During the trip, Swanson consumed two funnel cakes, a medium chocolate smoothie, and a large Dr. Pepper.

At press time, Swanson told reporters he was "super-motivated" in the New Year, and would probably do a couple of squats tomorrow, or maybe even a sprint to the local Chili's for lunch.

Chinese Hacker Complains About 'Perverted' American Military

By G-Had

BEIJING, China — According to Chinese news agencies, the head of a People's Liberation Army unit of military hackers is planning to file a formal complaint today with the U.S. Department of Defense after a number of what were called "disturbing" conversations with "American military perverts."

Senior Col. Bo Wang of the People's Glorious Facebook Battalion is one of thousands of Chinese military personnel who spend all-day attempting to infiltrate the social media profiles of US military and intelligence personnel with fake accounts.

Once a target is identified, the hacker will create a false profile, usually of an attractive member of the opposite sex, and 'friend' the target. Over time, a successful hacker can friend almost an entire unit and learn valuable information about military or intelligence plans.

The problem, as Wang soon found out, is that the majority of his targets are young American servicemen, most of whom only agree to friend requests because they expect sexual favors at some point.

"With a typical E-3 or E-4 target, I usually get requests to exchange naked pictures within the first week," said Wang. "At first I thought this was the easiest job in the world, but the requests kept getting more and more explicit. Last week I had a gunnery sergeant ask for a picture of me deep-throating a broken beer bottle."

Wang further complained about the frequently-graphic sexual requests he receives, which he blames on a society "over-saturated with pornography."

"Just because I am pretending to be a friendly girl doesn't mean you can ask me for a rim-job or say you're going to fuck me in half!"

To make matters worse, an alarming number of his targets are married.

"I'll have lance corporals posting pictures of them with their wives on their timeline while they're messaging me about finding a place to hook up. What's wrong with these people?"

Wang said the problem is not just confined to the enlisted ranks.

"I spoke to a 2nd Lt. Branum earlier this week, pretending to be a college girl from Texas A&M. All I said was 'Hello' and before I could say anything else, he asked if I would piss on his face!'"

"I can't believe he kisses his mother with that mouth!"

The final straw though, according to Wang, is that many of the women he encounters are just as bad if not worse than the men.

"I had a female petty officer with signals intelligence ask me to 'fist' her, which I later learned means shove my whole arm up her ass. I almost threw up afterwards."

Wang hopes his complaint will convince the Department of Defense to institute more sensitivity training, so that future espionage missions won't leave his men "dead to the world, eyes glazed over, with no hope for mankind."

"If I have to look at one more picture of a sailor holding his cock with the caption 'Permission to Come Aboard?' I'm going to lose it."

Terminal Lance Creator Revealed To Be Sergeant Major Of Marine Corps

By G-Had

CAMP LEJEUNE, N.C. — Enlisted Marines everywhere were stunned this week after learning that the creator of enlisted-life comic strip Terminal Lance is actually former Sgt. Maj. of the Marine Corps Carlton Kent.

The story broke after an alert data specialist at Camp Lejeune noticed that the IP address for the Terminal Lance website was actually the same one used by the retired sergeant major's work computer.

Upon being questioned by a Duffel Blog investigative reporter, Kent admitted that he had created the comic and was continuing to post weekly updates on the Terminal Lance website.

According to the sergeant major, he came up with the idea back in 2009 with then-Commandant, Gen. James Conway.

"We'd been getting a shitload of negative feedback over all the safety briefs we were subjecting our Marines to," said Kent. "I mean, you can only listen to so many of the fuckers before you just tune them out."

"But you devil dogs wanna keep crashing your brand-new crotch rocket motorcycles that you just bought with 18% APR and then killing yourselves after your wife leaves you cause you're 20 grand in the hole and eating dog food every night. So bottom line is we needed a new way to reach out."

"I said to Gen. Conway, 'man, it would be fucking great if we just had some comic that all the E-3's read, and we could just insert our messages into that.' Conway looks at me and says 'shit yeah, sergeant major, I think you've got something there.' And so the idea for Terminal Lance was born."

According to Kent, writing under a pen name was essential.

"No one's gonna listen to dumb ole' sergeant major, especially the sergeant major of the Marine Corps, but they will listen to a fellow lance corporal, so that's who I had to pretend to be. 'Maximilian Uriarte' is actually an anagram for 'Do Your Leading Marines MCI'. I'm amazed no one caught it earlier. Then we hired some combat camera guy as our front man and made a bunch of videos of him with his nuts hanging out."

While most of the strips are routine 'enlisted-life-sucks,' Kent does point to some key issues.

"Don't Ask Don't Tell was a big one," he says. "We had all kinds of polling saying that Marines were dead-set against repeal, and that doesn't make us look good. So we ran a strip saying the Marine Corps is already gay, so what's the difference if it's open? Then just before the repeal we put out a strip about how gay Marines wouldn't be letting our boots dress so stupid, because everybody hates a stupid boot. End result: we've got gay Marines serving loud and proud and no one's complaining!"

Kent said he was currently working on the recent media scandals involving Marines.

"We've got one where we make fun of all the bullshit Nazi-wannabes, because nothing changes behavior faster than public ridicule. We also did one after the pissing incident, where we just reminded Marines not to put shit on YouTube, because even I like to piss in a dead Taliban's mouth once in a while."

The retired sergeant major also detailed the possibility the strip might branch out to other ranks.

"Let's face it, we have a lot of stupid lieutenants out there. Maybe we can get Abe and Garcia a lieutenant who's a total jack-off and teach our lieutenants proper command techniques through him."

For all his success, Kent was unsure about the long-term survival of Terminal Lance.

"I've been trying to get Sgt. Maj. Barrett into it, but he just doesn't have the right mindset. He tried doing one the other day where Abe's feeling suicidal and calls the DStress hotline. Come on, you know that shit wouldn't happen," Kent said.

"Abe would call it because he's drunk dialing and winds up hitting on the operator, and says he's going to kill himself if she doesn't come over and blow him. Fuck, anything that gets Marines to put that number in their phone, right?"

BEHIND THE BLOG

Long before there was Duffel Blog, the only real military-focused humor site that was super popular was Terminal Lance. Started by Max Uriarte as a Marine infantry-focused comic strip, it was well-read throughout the Corps. Back in 2009, a common question among Marines — myself included — was, "hey did you see the latest Terminal Lance?"

Fast forward to 2012, with Duffel Blog just coming on the scene. One of the writers thought it would be hilarious to write an article that made it seem like the Sergeant Major of the Marine Corps was actually behind the entire thing. When this article originally published, it ended up blowing up, and it was passed around the Corps like wildfire.

When Max found out, he emailed me. All he said was, "Duffelblog, Touché." Later, Max and I ended up finally meeting and we became good friends, and we even kicked back a few beers with Sgt. Maj. Kent in San Francisco. Kent also thought the article was hilarious.

To this day, there are still Marines who seriously believe that Max is Sgt. Maj. Kent. Touché, indeed.

Blasting Shrill Whistle Throughout Ship Great For Morale, Navy Study Finds

By Drew Ferrol

NORFOLK, Va. — A surprising US Navy study recently found the greatest way to increase shipboard morale was to blast earsplitting whistles over the intercom at random intervals.

"We were surprised at the results," said Force Master Chief Rachel Michaels. "We thought better food or larger berthings would make sailors happier. Turns out the thing they like the most are whistles so loud they can cause pain."

"Our study found the only thing sailors like more than a boatswain's mate's whistle over the 1MC is sounds of pure feedback from the speakers at maximum volume," Michaels added, screaming over jet engine blasts on a carrier deck. "So we're going to try doing that too. We also expect all sailors to take our hearing conservation program seriously."

"Oh yeah, the whistles are great," said Aviation Ordnanceman 2nd Class Howard Davis. "At 0600 we get woken up by a whistle that's loud as hell, and it's followed by another one that's a minute-and-a-half long. It's the best way to start the morning. Throughout the day, they blast the whistles for no reason. I've heard the different sounds mean different things, and I'm trying my hardest to learn them. If I can't distinguish between a set of whistles and trills I might miss an important announcement."

"I've never heard any whistling on board," Boatswain's Mate 1st Class Jeff Kelly said when asked for comment. "It's called piping."

Kelly's face turned beet red and he began shouting orders to calm himself down. "Muster on the forecastle after chow! Stand at attention Seaman! It's not a fucking rope, it's a line!"

Unfortunately, Chief Michaels had to cut her interview with Duffel Blog short, saying she had an important task force on improving upon the well-received blue camouflage uniform.

"It's going to take us at least four years of research and a few hundred million dollars," Michaels said, "but we are working hard to fulfill our sailors' request to replace all pants zippers with thirteen button flaps."

Pentagon Study Finds Beards Directly Related To Combat Effectiveness

By Sgt B

TAMPA, Fla. — Forget new gear, weapons, or sophisticated targeting systems. The newest tool coming to combat troops is low-tech: Beards. In a report released yesterday, research think-tank Xegis Solutions noted that beards have a direct correlation to combat effectiveness.

Jonathon Burns was the lead researcher in the study.

"We took 100 soldiers. 25 were Special Forces qualified and had beards, 25 were Special Forces qualified without beards, 25 were regular Army allowed to grow beards for the study, and the last 25 were regular Army without beards. All 100 of these subjects were in direct combat in Afghanistan during the study."

He continued: "Xegis Solutions had several teams of researchers embedded with these troops to make observations on their combat effectiveness. The results were overwhelming: Out of the 50 soldiers with beards, zero were wounded or killed and they had a significantly higher accuracy of fire than the soldiers without beards. The soldiers lacking beards had a higher rate of weapons malfunctions and basically, shit went wrong most of the time."

US Central Command wasted no time establishing a new rule forcing males to grow beards. Commander Gen. James Mattis issued a statement to all troops in combat zones.

"The time has come for the armed forces to accept the facts, and the facts are that beards save lives. All this time it was speculated that Green Berets were better because of their superior and intensive training while in fact, most of it had to do with beards."

There's no doubt that many in the Special Forces community will be angered, but Mattis is convinced.

"It's settled science. In light of this information we will enforce a rule requiring all males to wear at least one inch of facial hair at all times. Furthermore, any females able to grow facial hair are encouraged to do so as well."

BEHIND THE BLOG

This was probably the first-ever "viral" Duffel Blog post. Something about it just clicked with readers. Perhaps it was having Mattis with a prominent role, but my guess is that this article was printed out and posted everywhere for soldiers and Marines trying to justify not having to shave.

"Oh come on, first sergeant! Don't you know that beards save lives?"

The story mentions a study by Xegis Solutions, which was not linked to, since it did not exist. One reader, named Sarah, emailed about this discrepancy: "I just saw the article posted on the Duffel Blog about Jonathan Burn's study of beards and military combat.... can you send me the link to your source? I would like to see the research paper."

About a week later, we sent her back a four-page PDF file, which was marked Classified with big red font. There was a bunch of hilarious bullshit in the first few pages, but the evidence page, which included photos of beardless and bearded versions of David Letterman and Conan O'Brien was the best part.

Caption: "Prebeard Conan O'Brien. Complete pussy."

For some strange reason, she never responded.

First Sergeant Gives 72-Hour-Long Weekend Liberty Brief

By Paul Sharpe

CAMP LEJEUNE, N.C. – Marine Corps officials are celebrating the efforts of the company first sergeant for Golf Co., 2nd Battalion, 6th Marines today, after his 72-hour long weekend liberty brief broke a streak of off-duty incidents that has plagued the unit.

This past weekend is the first incident-free weekend for the company in over six months.

"It's been really damn rough here, I'll tell you that," said 1st Sgt. Daniel Bowling. "These devil dogs just won't listen to me. The first sergeant is out here giving a libo brief and these idiots just go out and do the opposite. I knew I had to take a different track."

The first sergeant decided to modify the existing policy for securing Marines for their weekends off, which includes talks by the commanding officer, the first sergeant, platoon sergeants, squad leaders, fire team leaders, the family readiness officer, battalion chaplain, a representative from supply, and the Duty NCO's for the weekend.

"I really thought the SOP with everyone talking about libo pitfalls was ok, but the messages were getting mixed," said Bowling.

At approximately 4:30 p.m. last Friday, his Marines formed up outside the company headquarters.

"He started out with the standard fluff we always hear," said Cpl. Paul Sweizer. "You know, those zingers like 'Don't do anything I wouldn't do, and if you do, I ain't bailing your ass out. And for the love of God, don't name it after me.'"

Sources within the company reported that the first few hours of the first sergeant's brief were a laundry list of items his Marines should not be doing over the weekend. Items included having sex without a condom, drinking and driving, going to Mexico, having sex with prostitutes, having sex with the colonel's daughter, and drinking and driving without a condom on.

"These Marines are better off now that they know what I expect," said Bowling. "If I didn't tell them if you get VD, it's going to hurt when you piss, how are they gonna know? And when I was a young devil dog, I was told not to use power tools in the shower and it helped me so I just need to pass that knowledge on."

A squad leader in the company's 1st Platoon believed the efforts of the company's top enlisted leader were crucial.

"The fact is that we were having an incident every weekend, and typically it was something that no one had ever seen before," said Sgt. Raymond Ewing. "Last weekend the first sergeant mentioned just about everything under the sun, then some PFC bangs some tranny-hooker without a condom in a police parking lot. I mean come on!"

On Saturday morning, First Sergeant Bowling warned of the dangers of sexual relations with transvestite hookers without a condom.

"Hey gents, let's not go banging trannies in a parking lot of a damn police station! Where you at Morales?" asked Bowling, calling for Pfc. Juan Morales, who was still pending his non-judicial punishment for the previous incident. "Oh, and speaking of cops. Let's not punch police officers repeatedly in the face."

Other Marines reported more graphic depictions of sex acts and the ensuing pitfalls.

"Hey, don't be a dummy, cum on her tummy. We don't want to add or detract from the population this weekend," said Bowling, according to witnesses at the brief.

"He kept using these weird code words and innuendo," said Lance Cpl. Jeff Storm. "Stuff like 'if you're planning on sending rounds downrange, use a blank adaptor, because you don't want to get rodded off the range.'"

The sun began to rise on Monday morning, just as Bowling was saying, "If you have to make airplane noises to put it in her mouth, then she is too young, gents."

"Oh shit, looks like libo is secured. Alright, let's start off on a meritorious Monday," said Bowling. "Platoon sergeants, carry out the plan of the day."

BEHIND THE BLOG

This story, like many written at Duffel Blog, is based on true events. For me, the inspiration came from two sources: Then-1st Sgt. Sylvester Daniels, my company first sergeant at Weapons Co., 3rd Battalion, 3rd Marines, who told us every Friday to "wear a condom out there, whether you're with your girlfriend, your boyfriend, whatever the case may be."

The second source is a little wilder: It's a story I literally could not make up even if I tried.

When I was an instructor at the School of Infantry, I had a Marine sign out with his buddy on liberty, promptly ditch his libo buddy (that's bad), go and buy a car at around 37% interest (that's against the rules and stupid), drive it down to Mexico (not supposed to do that either), drink underage (that's not allowed), then bang a hooker (not good either) without a condom (are you fucking stupid?). He later drove drunk back across the border and crashed the car, and forgot where he crashed said car. He got a cab, and ended up showing up to Sunday formation about 30 minutes late.

Oh, and the little shit didn't even get a haircut.

And then there was the time I had two Marines drive to Mexico and drive back across the border in a van carrying illegal immigrants. I had the good fortune of taking the call from US Border Patrol.

So, if you're wondering why first sergeant won't stop babbling on about all the bad shit that you're not supposed to do out there… Well, let's just say he or she is covering their bases.

Company Commander Suffers Existential Crisis After Losing Green Notebook

By Frederick Taub

FORT BRAGG, N.C. — A company commander with Echo Co., 2nd Battalion, 505th Parachute Infantry Regiment has locked himself in his office and refused to come out after his psyche was apparently shattered by the loss of his treasured Federal Supply Service green notebook, sources confirmed Thursday.

"At first it was a normal day," said 1st Sgt. Joseph Quincy, standing near a group of concerned officers and soldiers gathered around Capt. Eugene Reilly's bolted door. "But then the CO started taking a little longer than usual coming out to PT formation. I mean, he's usually moseying out like five or 10 minutes late, but this was a little ridiculous."

Quincy told reporters the distraught commander finally came out to the company area "with a dead look in his eyes" and began mumbling.

"He just kept repeating 'It's over. It's gone.' Then the CO just sprints back into his office, slams the door and starts crying."

According to Executive Officer Lt. Patrick Conrad, who carried on a brief conversation with the stricken commander through the window, Reilly has succumbed to a Dadaesque epiphany of the futility of life and the fallen nature of the world.

Notes on unit letterhead retrieved by Duffel Blog that Reilly reportedly shoved through the crack under his door contain scribbled verses of tormented absurdist prose, sketches of evanescent green notebooks being implacably torn apart by the vengeful talons of memory, and quotes from Dostoyevsky's The Brothers Karamazov.

Fortunately for all involved, Spc. Karl Bradley had recently gone through a mandatory two-day interactive Applied Suicide Intervention Skills Training (ASIST). He managed to stabilize the situation by asking the company commander if he was planning on killing himself. This sent Reilly into a verbose circumlocutory on man's futile search for meaning he had gleaned from Myth of Sisyphus.

The temporary setback was only halted when Bradley, in a valiant attempt to save his superior, poked his anti-suicide Act, Care, Escort (ACE) card underneath the door.

Upon reception of the card Capt. Reilly shrieked, "if God is dead, all is permitted!" before hurling himself out of his first story office window.

Google Street View Team Hits IED In Kandahar, 2 Killed

By Maxx Butthurt

KANDAHAR, AFGHANISTAN – The Global War on Terror claimed new casualties this week, though the victims were not Afghan civilians or U.S. military personnel.

Two American civilians were killed and one wounded when their Google Street View Prius triggered an IED while driving the streets of southern Afghanistan.

With the much-publicized U.S. pullout from Afghanistan looming on the horizon, the State Department had urged American businesses and private investors to continue to support the fledgling democracy. Touting a decrease in violent attacks across the nation, the White House had encouraged U.S. mapping companies to update their Afghanistan databases, giving greater access and understanding about the third-world nation to the rest of the world.

Google was the first company to respond, sending a team to begin street-level input in the major southern Afghan city of Kandahar, once called the heartland of the Taliban, and still home to over 40,000 U.S. and Coalition military personnel actively engaged in combat operations.

"Our mission with Google Street View has always been to show people places that they would never get off their lazy ass and be able to see otherwise," said Robert Smith, a spokesman for the company.

Unfortunately for the mapping team, led by veteran Google employee John Volstead, the country was not nearly as quiet or subdued as the US government had led them to believe.

After paying five different bribes to Afghan officials, police officers, and one 12-year-old boy with an AK-47 who claimed that he "owned the alley" that the team was trying to drive through, the team arrived at their first location, just 50 meters south of an Afghan National Army combat outpost. The uniformed Afghans, munching on MREs and other American-provided staples, sat on the HESCO parapets of their base and watched the crew intently, ignoring passing traffic and weapon-laden vehicles that cruised openly past the location.

Moments after the Google team exited their vehicle, the crew's Afghan driver bolted from the scene, leaving them alone, confused, and without an interpreter. Undaunted, Volstead began to set up his equipment, and ordered his team to do the same.

Those routine actions were interrupted when rookie member Wanda Folkes, a University of California-Berkeley graduate, anti-war activist, and former Peace Corps volunteer, stepped on a pressure plate IED, killing her and a passerby instantly and wounding two other members of the group. As Volstead began screaming for help, the Afghan soldiers, all of whom were on cellphones or holding up cheap video cameras, ignored his cries and continued to watch the scene.

"There was a serious bomb that just went off," said ANA Sgt. Muhammed Atollah as he uploaded the video to his YouTube account. "We're in the military. We don't have the training to respond to such things."

Afghan children began searching the smoking crater for trinkets or valuables that Folkes may have dropped.

Eventually a U.S. Army unit arrived to secure the scene, treating the remaining casualties and berating the ANA troops for their lack of action. In response, the men asked the U.S. soldiers for more water and extra batteries for their video cameras, which they had exhausted while filming the IED strike.

When told about the Google team's mission and reason for being in the area, U.S. Army platoon sergeant Miles Wallace said of the incident: "Well that's fucking stupid."

Texas Marine Refuses To Annoy Others By Telling Them Where He's From

By Jack Mandaville

CAMP PENDLETON, Calif. — Marines from the lone star state are enraged today after reports emerged indicating that one of their own does not relentlessly announce his Texas heritage to everyone within earshot.

Lance Cpl. Stuart G. Shaw, a rifleman with 1st Light Armored Reconnaissance Battalion, is receiving unfriendly fire after it was revealed that he was a native Texan — something he failed to announce on his own. Shaw, who was born and raised in San Marcos, Texas, says the whole controversy is being blown out of proportion.

"This has been really rough on me and my family," says the 21-year-old. "All of my fellow Texans have shut me out. They hiss at me when I walk past. They call me 'traitor' and 'sellout.' Some have even thrown their empty Shiner bottles at me. I don't know where all this hate is coming from."

The controversy started after Shaw and a group of other Marines went out to a local bar and were asked to present identification. As Shaw pulled out his ID, a fellow Marine spotted the Texas driver's license and word quickly spread.

"That dog just won't hunt," says Cpl. Robby Garcia of Stanton. "That kid would steal the nickels off a dead man's eyes. He's so low you'd need a coal mine railroad to find him. He has been in the Marine Corps for over two years and never bothered no one about being from Texas. I tell you what, man. As a dang ol' Texan, it is not only our right, but our duty to shove our heritage in peoples' faces. Now, if you will excuse me, I have some high school football to watch."

Yet Shaw has found support from many non-Texans.

"If you ask me, I think the kid is a pioneer," says Sgt. Will Giancarlo of Lacrosse, Wis., a member of Shaw's platoon. "You don't see people from Vermont constantly making maple syrup money shots on people. I mean, I always had my suspicions about him, ya know? He really liked going to The Stampede on libo and always called everybody sir or ma'am. But other than that, he was a normal guy. People need to leave him alone."

That's not good enough according to Jeff Wilbanks, Shaw's team leader and a native of Odessa, Texas.

"I just don't understand how he could stab us in the back like that," says Wilbanks. "We all feel betrayed. He could have hung a gigantic Texas flag in his barracks room. He could have gotten a Texas-themed tattoo."

"I've got a message for Shaw," he says as he lifts up his shirt and shows off his Texas flag tattoo on his chest. "You see that? It means, 'Not welcome!'"

BEHIND THE BLOG

If you're confused by this story, it's only because you've never met a person from Texas.

You'll know any time you meet someone from Texas, since they'll tell you within the first minute of conversation. They're almost as bad as Navy SEALs.

Citing OPSEC Fears, DoD Bans Tapout Clothing for All Military Personnel

By Ron

WASHINGTON, D.C. — Citing concerns over operational security, the Department of Defense has implemented a policy prohibiting all military personnel from wearing Tapout clothing, including t-shirts, hats, and accessories, when out of uniform.

The new policy went into effect Thursday on the recommendation of a council led by Dr. James Miller, principal deputy undersecretary of defense for policy.

"Even though Tapout gear is incredibly tacky, that's not what this is about," Miller said in a press conference. "Admittedly, as a mixed martial arts enthusiast, I take personal issue with fat soldiers walking around with 'Tapout' on their chest, when they can't skip rope for five minutes, let alone step in a locked cage against a trained fighter. And to me, whether you're fat or fit, if you don't know the difference between an omoplata and a gogoplata, then you just look like a jerk in a Tapout shirt. But at the end of the day, we're primarily looking at our troops' safety."

Miller stressed that the ban stems from concerns about Tapout gear and operational security, or OPSEC. According to a DoD press release, OPSEC is defined as "seemingly harmless information that adversaries can use to develop intelligence against our forces."

Miller said that officials were concerned that Tapout clothing "could give the enemy a big-picture idea of how many military personnel are in an area, where they go in their off time, and what kind of asinine garbage they spend on their money on. Basically, if I go to a movie theater and see a bunch of Tapout shirts, I know two things: one, there must be a base nearby, and two, with all these posers around, I'm probably the best fighter there, pound for pound."

Miller said that a defense working group was sent to San Diego, California, Fayetteville, North Carolina, Jacksonville, North Carolina, and San Antonio, Texas to observe people in Tapout gear. The group went to shopping centers, bars, and Dave & Busters, and asked people wearing Tapout clothing whether they were in the military. The working group's data indicates that 1 percent of the people interviewed were civilian mixed martial artists, 15 percent were local douchebags, and 84 percent were active-duty military.

"84 percent is a big deal," Miller said. "Even though this wasn't a formal study, we can't sit by and do nothing. Not too long ago, I went to a mall outside of Joint Base Lewis-McChord on a Friday night and thought I was in the middle of a UFC Fan Expo. And I'm willing to bet dollars to donuts that not one of those guys could throw a switch kick, or counter a basic double leg, or maintain an appropriate range against a fighter with a reach advantage. Also, don't forget the OPSEC."

Many military personnel are not pleased.

"This is bullshit," said Spc. Frank Alvarado, a soldier assigned to the 82nd Airborne Division at Ft. Bragg. "I wear Tapout because it's an expression of who I am. I'm a soldier, but I also train UFC."

Miller said that the working group will be sent out to identify other possible OPSEC concerns, such as skin-tight Under Armour workout shirts worn at bars and restaurants, high-and-tight haircuts, and civilian wives so overweight they make the passenger side of the couple's Honda Civic dip when they get in.

BEHIND THE BLOG

This article had great feedback when it was first published. While plenty of people got the joke, the funniest reactions came from people who regularly don Tapout gear and were super pissed thinking they could no longer wear it.

The best reaction, however, came from a military public affairs officer. The officer tweeted at the Duffel Blog account and said (paraphrasing), "number of people calling to complain about DoD banning Tapout gear: 1, and that's too many."

Then there was an article written in Yell Magazine by Shawn Loeffler, who was quite angered by quotes from Dr. James Miller.

"Dr. James Miller is a biased dick with some kind of vendetta or score to settle," he wrote. "Maybe mommy didn't give him enough attention. Maybe he got his ass kicked throughout high school. Maybe he feels his MMA skills are underappreciated."

Yes, that's right. Loeffler didn't "get it." And yes, that article at Yell Magazine is still online. Google that shit.

Soldier Hospitalized After Masturbating With CLP

By Hammer Lip

FORT CAMPBELL, Ky. — After complaining that his "dick pipe closed up," Pvt. Eric Draughter was admitted to Blanchfield Army Community Hospital early Wednesday where he was diagnosed with having Cleaner, Lubricant, and Protectant (CLP) in his urethra.

"CLP, a solvent for stripping firing residue from weapons, is not meant for human consumption or use as a personal lubricant," said Dr. Russell Beckham, while holding back tears of what was likely laughter.

A source at Blanchfield told Duffel Blog that Draughter could barely walk when he stumbled through the emergency room doors around 2:00 am on Wednesday.

"We all thought he snorted too much Viagra and had a four-hour red rocket. Boy, were we wrong," said the source. The source brought Draughter into an examination room where the young soldier dropped his JNCO jeans and began to frantically tell an incoherent story about how he was "rubbing one out to some barracks cooze with gun lube."

The source reported that Draughter used CLP as lubricant because one of his squad mates said it would lead to a "good release."

As is Blanchfield protocol, Draughter was rodded for 30 minutes in order to clear the blockage during which he lost consciousness three times.

"Draughter will make a full recovery after a week of soreness and painful urination," the source said. The source went on to say that Draughter had been put on a three-week "no crank down profile" and that the entire Medical Protection System malfunctioned after updating his file.

"God damnit, why couldn't that kid use spit like everyone else?" said 1st Sgt. Stephen Doucer, the soldier's company first sergeant. "You gotta be fist fucking me with this numbskull." Sources said Doucer later muttered under his breath about wanting to suck-start his M4 and then proceeded to write down notes for Friday's upcoming safety brief on safe personal lubricants.

At press time, the brigade commander was seeking a compassionate reassignment for Draughter, after concluding that "no one would want to go to a war with a kid who can't even jerk off correctly."

BEHIND THE BLOG

I'd just like to make it clear that I have never masturbated with CLP.

Military Spouse Gets Chip Bag Stuck On Its Head

By Ron

AUGUSTA, Ga. — The spouse of a Fort Gordon soldier is breathing easier after a military police officer removed a Doritos bag from its head.

Several witnesses reported to law enforcement officials that they saw the spouse wandering on lawns in base housing with a family-sized Doritos bag over its head and flailing its arms.

"I tried to run over to help," said Sgt. 1st Class Tom Wilkins, an area resident, "but it disappeared into the woods before I could get there."

The spouse was spotted later in the day in the PX parking lot by a worker out collecting shopping carts.

"I hate to see this," said the employee, Ernesto Macapagal. "It hurts my heart to see them when they suffer."

Macapagal was too afraid to approach the spouse himself, so he reported the incident to his manager, who then called MPs.

Police Commander Maj. Harold Alonzo said the spouse allowed the officer to remove the bag without a struggle.

Military spouses are usually docile and content to remain in their habitats, but are known to venture out of their territory when hungry or during mating seasons, such as the middle of a unit's deployment cycle, according to a publication from the U.S. Fish and Wildlife Service.

While once rare for a spouse to leave a house with a chip bag stuck on its head, Alonzo said that with buy-one-get-one-free sales going on at the commissary, he now sees this exact same incident happen two or three times a week.

"I wish I was able to ask it what happened," Alonzo said, "but my best guess is that it was startled by something it saw on Maury."

"I suppose we're lucky that the smell of nacho cheese helped keep it relatively calm," Alonzo added.

The spouse was taken to the base veterinary clinic, where it was spayed, tagged, and released back to base housing. It has apparently made a full recovery and gone back to its daily routine, as it has been spotted driving a 2013 GMC Terrain reportedly purchased with deployment paychecks.

Upon being notified of the incident and threatened with a fine if it happens again, the deployed soldier instructed MPs to capture the beast and euthanize it.

Typo Leads To Creation Of $179 Million Gorilla Warfare Program

By Dark Laughter

CRESCENT CITY, Calif. — The Department of Defense has confirmed accusations that a $179 million military training program for mountain gorillas was created based on a spelling error in an email between two high-ranking Army officers, according to official sources.

The admission follows more than a year of denials, which were originally sparked by a leaked copy of the email from an anonymous whistleblower.

"As these large wars end and we refocus on the possibility of proxy wars with China over resources and influence in the Pacific, South America, and Africa, we need to think about putting a small scale Green Beret-like capability in at least a few of our regular infantry battalions," the email begins.

"This is partly just a recruiting ploy to put in the commercials, but it would also identify local talent that we could pull out of gen pop and send to Camp Mackall or the Rangers. God bless the SEALs and Marines, but they're the only things standing between the goddamn Navy and total irrelevancy. Screw [the Goldwater-Nichols Act of 1986], we need more special forces and shock troops to price them out of the market. To stand up that kind of capability, we'll need to budget for a new gorilla [sic] warfare program."

The email soon came to the attention of Adm. William McRaven, commander of the U.S. Special Operations Command. Unfortunately, the email seems to have only been forwarded in part, and McRaven saw just the final three sentences, which he forwarded to Chief of Naval Operations Adm. Jonathan Greenert.

A week later, Secretary of the Navy Ray Mabus, accompanied by Greenert and caged silverback mountain gorilla Ojore, publicly announced that the Navy's Marine Mammal Program would, "like the Navy SEALs and Marines, now expand to cover threats on sea, air, and land, and in any clime and place," a statement now believed to have been intended to provoke the Army based on Mabus' mistaken impression of the email.

Despite originally having no interest in actual gorillas, the Army complained that the Navy had no business in what was logically an Army mission, since there was nothing aquatic about gorillas. The Navy, concerned that they might be completely shut out of the military gorilla field, responded that 'marine mammal' was a description of the animals' training, not their natural habitat, and threatened to press for takeover of the Army's working dog program since the Army routinely teaches their dogs how to swim. Following a period of bitter bureaucratic infighting, the Army grudgingly backed down and created their own gorilla program with a similar level of funding.

A compromise between the two services was negotiated soon after by Rep. Mike Thompson (D-Calif.) of the House Ways and Means Committee, an Army veteran and a "strong believer in the military gorilla concept."

Thompson's compromise produced the Joint Military Gorilla Program (JMGP), which combined the Army and Navy's gorilla programs in a single $100 million facility headquartered outside Crescent City, California, and also created a prestigious liaison billet for an Air Force officer.

The location of the facility in what was then-Thompson's home district led to allegations of corruption and pork-barrel spending, at which point WikiLeaks received and published the original email along with several hundred related emails from later in the project's development.

The scandal died down when JMGP spokesman and head primatologist Dr. Warren Reed explained that California's 1st District contained one of only a few cloud forest habitats in the U.S., which was vital for proper gorilla research, and that this, combined with factors such as proximity to the ocean and other regional military facilities, made it the only possible choice. The story then faded until a sharp-eyed reader, outspoken military reformer Col. Roy Casey, USAF (Ret.), looked at the initial email, realized the misunderstanding, and posted the entire story on his blog, which was soon picked up by both Wired and Foreign Policy. Interest in the story immediately revived, and the Department of Defense's denials began.

"I think this tells you a lot about the culture of the DoD," said Casey. "There was no reality check anywhere in the chain that offered even a single question about this, even as simple a question as 'sir, did you mean guerrilla warfare?' Never mind questions about the number of gorillas left in the world, the difficulty of teaching military science to animals only capable of sign language, or the dangers of handling even a single wild fucking gorilla, much less how those dangers might be compounded if you gathered a large group of gorillas in one place, armed them, and then trained them how to operate as a military unit. People were either too afraid or too stupid to ask their bosses hard questions. This is even worse than the Bradley."

By 'worse than the Bradley,' Casey is referring to problems of corruption and incompetence that plagued the development of the Army's Bradley Fighting Vehicle, and which were exposed by his fellow military reformer Col. James Burton in the book *The Pentagon Wars*.

However, Dr. Reed is pleased with the program's results.

"The critics can say whatever they want, but we're seeing real progress. The mountain gorilla social hierarchy maps perfectly onto a military hierarchy, and these guys have a passion for learning. It took very little time to get them up to reading children's books, and after only a few months they'd moved on to history. And as soon as Petty Officer Ojore reads a book, he hands it off to his Army counterpart, Sgt. Munyiga, then on down the line until they've all finished it. One week it will be The Spartacus War. The next week it will be Mutiny on the Amistad. Sure, sometimes they get confused, like when Ojore signed that he wanted a copy of Alberto Bayo's 150 Questions for a Guerrilla, but he played it off and made a big show of reading it cover to cover anyway."

"As far as Col. Casey, his claims are ridiculous," said Reed. "The truth is; we have no problem admitting when we make mistakes or have setbacks. For instance, while the subjects have picked up reading very quickly, we've been disappointed with their sign language. During the day, they seem able to sign normally, but at night their signs to each other are nonsense, just hours of back and forth nonsense."

Casey remains unconvinced.

"What's worse than this error making it so long without getting caught is that, even when the error finally came to light, they chose to double down on the mistake instead of correcting it. It's like the F-35. 'Hey, we're so delusional that we believe even our complete fuck-ups are somehow accidentally brilliant.' Don't get me wrong...screw WikiLeaks, fuck that twerp Assange, and Manning should get ten lashes on the National Mall. But the fact is that this shows the DoD still has brain cancer. Until they institutionalize reform processes instead of sending their white blood cells after anyone who tries to handle reform in-house, they'll need someone outside getting in their soup to keep them honest. Looking at this mess, you've got to wonder just how badly things would have to go wrong before they'd admit they screwed up."

Meanwhile, outside Crescent City, the program continues.

When questioned about a second WikiLeaks document which claimed that, following a month long cultural awareness course, the 12 silverbacks' behavior appeared to indicate that they had adopted a particularly radical type of Salafi Islam, the DoD refused to comment, except to vow that they would prosecute all involved in leaking the document.

Soldier Buffs Floor With Skill Of Casanova Penetrating A Young Venetian Handmaiden

By Armydave

FORT LEONARD WOOD — At two o'clock this morning, Spc. James Harrison buffed the battalion floor with a finesse reminiscent of the famed Italian amore, Giacomo Casanova, seducing an inexperienced young servant girl.

Harrison, much like the suave Italian lover, began with the subtle sounds of Vivaldi's Spring Concerto No. 1 in E Major. As the violin concerto bounced off the thickly painted walls, Harrison soothed a thick and slippery handful of wax across the tile floor. With a practiced hand and reassuring whispers, the young man worked the wax — his strong fingers grinding in small circular motions.

Reaching around, he became suddenly firm, nearly violent, and pushed the wax evenly into the floor — akin to the Italian flesh conqueror tossing his new prize, with a domineering force, onto an 18th century down comforter.

His game, wet and open, awaited his machine, and Harrison obliged. As Casanova would slide his hand up a new lover's thigh and rest her ankle on his shoulder, so too, did Specialist Harrison. The long yellow electrical cord hung over his right shoulder, draped serpentine down the hall, and plugged into a broken wall socket.

Then arose a click and a deep vibrating hum. As Harrison rocked the buffer back and forth, it throttled gently against the floor. With expert hands, he guided the buffer to penetrate deep into the surface of the tile. Oscillations ground and smothered the floor's porous surface with glistening wax.

What began with gentle caresses reached a fever pitch as Harrison swung the buffer to and fro, lost in a hurricane of hot musk and wax. The air hung with noise, much akin to the din of pleasure screams emitted by Casanova's numerous lovers.

Soon thereafter, Harrison threw a towel on the floor, walked outside to catch a smoke, then returned to the duty desk to answer phone calls.

None witnessed the affair except the gods of lust, the nymphs of the forest, and pictures of 4th Brigade's chain of command. Harrison nodded knowingly, yet comfortingly, confident in his understanding of the nuances of love and buffing.

Navy SEALs To Infiltrate Libya In Secret Mission, Major Book Publisher Reports

By Smelly Infidel

VIRGINIA BEACH, Va. — A major publisher of Navy SEAL memoirs reported today that a U.S. retaliation strike is "imminent" in Libya. Following the news stories of the attack on the U.S. Consulate in Benghazi, Libya, Random Day spokesman Bill Klein stated that several of their company's clients called with a preliminary manuscript for possible books.

"The first to contact us was Steve Faulkner," Klein said. "He is with DEVGRU... you know, the SEAL Team 6 guys. Anyway, he called us up late at night and said he wanted to present a new book idea for his autobiography, which would include several chapters on raids against terrorist camps in the Libyan desert."

Klein said the conversation was cut short because Faulkner stated that he would be leaving the next morning and would be gone for a while, possibly for several weeks.

"OPSEC is so important to these guys," said Klein, "so usually when a world event happens and they have to go respond, they'll have to quickly send us a manuscript for their next book idea before they get on a plane to go and do an op."

When Klein was asked about his usage of military slang, he was more than happy to answer.

"These operators and I have become so tight over the past several years. What, with all that's been going on and the slew of book ideas and manuscripts we've been reviewing, I've even opened up a satellite office in Virginia Beach just to handle all the material coming out of Dam Neck and Little Creek alone. The public affairs office over at Naval Special Warfare and I have developed a really good relationship, too."

Klein was happy to show reporters from the Duffel Blog other manuscripts sent in.

"This one here was from a young lieutenant over at Eight... that's SEAL Team 8," Klein said with a grin. "The working title is 'Into the Den of the Ayatollah,' but we're thinking of changing that."

Klein stated that he hasn't been able to contact the lieutenant because his unit shipped to the Persian Gulf a month ago.

"I expect he'll update his Facebook page soon with his location so that all his fans can follow him," Klein stated. The publisher has high hopes for the book, especially when the U.S. strikes at Iran's nuclear facilities later this year.

Duffel Blog reporters were fortunate to have Chief Petty Officer (SEAL) Bud Jorgenson show up with a manuscript during the interview with Klein. He was excited to talk about his experiences and get his name out there "to generate some buzz."

"Yeah, we get a quick class towards the end of BUD/S on how to write a good manuscript," Jorgenson said. "It's just as important to us as learning how to navigate underwater or conduct CQB. Once you get here to Virginia Beach though, one of the guys on the teams will introduce you to Bill here and really get your shit rolling. Of course, you have to get out on some ops first… some deployments under your belt, that sort of thing. Nobody wants fiction when they can read the real deal."

Klein stated that he is currently looking at the possibility of expanding Random Day's office in Virginia Beach.

"So many of the guys want to do movies, especially after 'Act of Valor' came out," Klein said. "Lots of guys were jealous of the trim the 'Act of Valor' SEALs were getting at the premier parties and such. It's way better than just being a wealthy book writer. I mean, what chick wants to bang an author? Being an actor is where it's really at."

Klein said he's currently in talks with Tri-Star and Paramount to open film studios in the Virginia Beach area.

Halfway Heroes, 'Near Veterans' Seek Recognition For Almost Serving In Military

By Dirty

CHARLESTON, S.C. — Jody Siever spends his Friday nights like so many American servicemen and women, mingling while kicking back drinks at a local bar. Recognizing the giveaway military haircut of a fellow patron, he approaches with an arm extended.

"Welcome home, soldier." Smiling, though apparently puzzled, the stranger returns a firm, brief handshake.

"Thanks, but I'm in the Navy. And I haven't been anywhere—I'm in Nuke School," he replies, referring to the Naval Nuclear Power Training Center in Goose Creek, S.C.

"That's cool," Siever says, "I almost thought about joining the Navy for a while, but if I did join the service, I would have gone into the Army. I'm just kind of hardcore like that. Shooting bad guys in the face — that's the life for me. If I wanted it."

Siever, you see, never actually enlisted.

Veteran service members often find it difficult to relate their experiences in the military to friends and family back home, but a new civilian organization is working to expand that exclusive brotherhood. The Bros Before Joes campaign, established in 2011, seeks to legitimize the efforts of people like Siever, whose commitments to serving in the military range from the hypothetical to the nearly realized.

"We've got guys from all over the spectrum here. Some of our members, they merely thought about joining the Army a few times, or took the ASVAB in high school to get out of first period," explains BBJ founder Trent Bower. "Other guys though, they got as far as making appointments to go to MEPS [Military Entrance Processing Station], but then something important came up."

A near-Marine himself, Bower recounts his own brush with fate:

"I talked with a Marine recruiter a few times in high school, even attended a couple of pool functions at the recruiting office. It got to the point that I was there so often, the recruiters even started calling me 'Boot.' They were practically begging me to enlist, but I always knew I was meant for something more meaningful."

Bower, a 31-year old assistant manager at a successful pizza delivery franchise, started the Bros Before Joes campaign in his spare time, seeking to bring recognition to others who share his story. For Siever, and thousands of almost-soldiers, sailors, airmen, and Marines like him, the organization is a long-overdue ray of hope.

Says Siever, "It's great, you know, to finally be able to reach out and connect with others who share your non-experiences. After giving so much, dedicating so much time and energy to thinking about enlisting, it just feels like we're finally getting the thanks we deserve." And recognition has been swift in coming.

Thanks to a successful joint-lobbying campaign with the Almost Iraq and Afghanistan Veterans of America, a bill is now before the Senate to approve Veteran's Affairs benefits for BBJ and AIAVA members. The resolution received overwhelming bipartisan support in a House vote earlier this year from a majority of US Representatives who are themselves non-veterans.

Regarding the passage in the House, Rep. Jeff Flake (R-Ariz.) released this statement:

"This isn't a Red-or-Blue, liberal-versus-conservative issue. It's about giving near-veterans like me and many of my constituents the recognition we've been denied for far too long." Currently, 345 out of 435, or roughly 80% of members of the U.S. House of Representatives, have no recorded military service.

As the bill nears the Senate floor, however, some opponents are voicing concerns. Senator and Navy veteran John McCain (R-Ariz.) held a press conference outside his home in Phoenix, Arizona on Tuesday, calling the bill "a mockery... of all that I hold dear."

He also stated that he would "rather tongue-kiss Jane Fonda" than vote to approve the measure. Before he could take questions, he had to be ushered away for medical treatment when blood began seeping from his clenched fist—reportedly from clutching his Silver Star too tightly.

And he's not alone. Sen. Daniel K. Inouye (D-Hawaii) is an Army veteran of World War II and presently the only serving member of Congress to have earned a Congressional Medal of Honor. When presented with the bill's full text, Sen. Inouye declared it "a perversion of our American values," and refused to touch it, even with his prosthetic arm. Said Inouye, "I don't want to live on this planet anymore."

Despite these protests, the bill has mass appeal with civilians and near-veterans on both sides of the aisle. Arguments will begin in earnest when the Senate reconvenes next January. Until then, it's a long wait for near-heroes like Siever and Bower.

Asked if he would do anything different given the opportunity, Bower harkens back to his non-Marine days:

"I just couldn't leave all of this behind. I miss those pool functions, though. They were good times; some of the best times of my life. You just... you go through something like that, almost sacrificing so much, with such a close group of guys, and it really makes you brothers, you know? I even think I still have some recruitment brochures around here, somewhere."

ISAF Drops Candy To Afghan Children, Kills 51

By G-Had

MAZAR-I-SHARIF, AFGHANISTAN – In a tragic accident earlier today, aircraft belonging to the International Security Assistance Force inadvertently killed 51 Afghans near the city of Mazar-i-Sharif while attempting to drop candy to a group of children.

According to accounts from both Afghans and international observers, two NATO aircraft, later identified as American C-130s, made a low pass over a village of several hundred Afghans outside the city.

Approximately 1.4 million M&Ms were to be delivered via Container Delivery System in a single package with a weight of 1500 lbs. Due to a malfunction in the static line, the parachute failed to deploy and the container crashed through the roof of a local school at nearly 100 miles per hour.

Upon impact, the force of the rapidly settling candies caused the sides to explode outward, causing what physics professor Dr. Rosella Schwartz described as "essentially a 360 degree anti-personnel mine full of chocolate flechettes."

By "flechettes," Schwartz is referring to the M&Ms' candy shells, which shattered and spalled upon entering the bodies of the victims and also caused more numerous and severe secondary injuries.

Dr. Manuel Velez of the Red Cross, one of the first medical personnel at the site of the impact, had a similar assessment of the candy shells' damage.

"I've seen a lot of injuries inflicted on civilians by military ordnance, but this was much worse," Velez said, stooping to change the bandages on one of the victims while pointing out the many blue, green, and yellow splotches.

"The worst were the peanut M&Ms. The soft chocolate acted as a sabot around the peanuts, so basically these things were candy-coated penetrator rounds."

ISAF spokesperson Col. Mark Marshall, who spoke to reporters today at a press conference in Kabul, said the candy drop was only the latest phase of a new operation called "Reese's for Peaces." He added that while ISAF regrets the accidental loss of civilian life, it would not deter them working to relieve the suffering of the Afghan people.

Sources at ISAF headquarters in Kabul said the operation was first proposed by Deputy Commander Gen. Bill Whitehead as a way to help boost the morale of Afghans as western forces began their long-anticipated drawdown.

Whitehead said he first got the idea after reading a book about the 1948 Berlin Airlift. After finishing their cargo deliveries, American pilots would drop pieces of candy to impoverished children, which earned the United States a lot of good publicity.

"Counterinsurgency is all about winning the hearts and minds of the people," said Whitehead, "and as we transition to a much smaller footprint, the Air Force is going to have to take on some of the roles traditionally filled by soldiers, such as handing out candy."

In early March, Whitehead gave ISAF the authority to begin planning a series of humanitarian airdrops over population centers in Afghanistan. Operation "Reese's for Peaces," referred to informally as "Dessert Storm", was launched two weeks later with MQ-9 Reapers dropping several tons of licorice on Kandahar.

Over the next few weeks, ISAF warplanes dropped tons of assorted chocolates, sweets, and even ice cream over the war-torn country. Other NATO countries also took part, with French planes dropping bon bons and German planes dropping Bavarian chocolate. The United States, however, is contributing the bulk of the candy being used in the operation.

The incident in Mazar-i-Sharif is unfortunately not the first setback for "Reese's for Peaces."

Other blunders included a crate-load of Baby Ruth bars being dropped short of its target on March 19 and plowing into a bus full of madrassa students, killing 22. On April 27, several Snickers bars hit a wedding party near Kunduz, killing 35. And on May 8, several packs of Starburst inadvertently hit an orphanage and killed 8 children and an adorable kitten named Mittens.

Following the press conference, Col. Marshall tried to exit the podium, but tripped and crashed into a group of civilians, killing 9.

Duffel Blog investigative writer Dark Laughter also contributed to this report.

Entire Battalion Flattened By 7-Ton After Road Guard Fails To Post

By Stormtrooper

CAMP PENDLETON, Calif. — The rhythmic echoes of running cadence are a familiar sound on any military installation, but the usual "lo-right-lay-oh" was accompanied by screams last Friday when an entire battalion was run over by a 7-Ton truck after a road guard failed to assume his post.

The Marines of 9th Communications Battalion are known for their penchant to engage in "boots and utes" battalion runs every Friday morning, led by their Battalion Commander, Col. Randall "Randy" Walker. Normally, formations are preceded by a pair of "road guards" wearing reflective vests to prevent vehicles from entering the roadway as the Marines run by.

However, when Walker shouted for road guards to "post" on the intersection they were about to pass through, one of the designated road guards, Private First Class Daniel Goodman, couldn't hear him over the cadence call and remained in formation.

Cpl. Nicholas Farina, a Motor Vehicle Operator with 7th Engineering Support Battalion, was towing a generator to a field exercise when he suddenly found himself bouncing over the bodies of the men and women of 9th Comm.

"I was just driving along 17th Street towards the FEX [sic] when I came upon an intersection. I looked both ways and saw a large group of Marines running towards me but they didn't post a road guard, so I assumed I was okay to drive," said Farina in his official statement of the tragedy. "The next thing I know, blood is spraying across my windshield."

According to forensic reports, the 7-Ton collided with the squad leaders while going roughly 30mph and just kept on going. Farina will not be facing charges for the deaths of nearly a hundred Marines, however, as Pfc. Goodman failed to indicate that there was a formation nearby and that it was unsafe to enter the roadway.

"Posting a road guard is crucial to the survival of Marines during formation runs," said Safety Officer Mrs. Lizette Horton, the civilian in charge of ensuring the battalion is always in compliance with Department of Defense safety protocols.

"Without a road guard in the street, it is sometimes impossible for motorists to notice a formation right in front of them. Despite the fact that each individual Marine wore a reflective belt around their waist or hydration system, it is very plausible that Corporal Farina didn't see them — which is why it is so important that a Marine in a full reflective vest stand in front of the oncoming traffic and not allow them to pass."

Currently, the three surviving Marines of 9th Communications Battalion, who were not present due to being on light duty, are engaged in a safety stand-down.

General's Controversial Graduation Speech Sparks Riots, 11 Killed

By Maxx Butthurt

SAND HILL, FT. BENNING, Ga. — Many soldiers and family members are angry over reports of controversial remarks from the Commanding Officer of Fort Benning at a recruit graduation.

Speaking to an assembled crowd of new soldiers and their families at basic training graduation, Maj. Gen. Robert Brown was reported as "extremely hostile."

His speech began with the "standard fluff" about duty, country, and the privileges of serving when such a small percentage of the country chooses a career in the Armed Forces. The speech took a turn, however, when the general reached a point in his remarks, obviously reused from previous ceremonies.

"Look to your left and right towards your brothers in arms," said Brown. "You're all now members of a proud warrior class, and heroes like your fathers before you who-"

The general stopped, took a deep breath and crumpled the sheet before flinging it to the ground.

"Fuck it! I can't read shit like this anymore. Listen up you little bald bastards."

The newly minted soldiers — trying to stay awake throughout the ceremony — shifted uncomfortably in their seats at the sudden change in tone.

"Some of you fucks won't make it past [Advanced Individual Training]. You'll wash out with the rest of the weakness that never should have been here in the first place. Most of you who do graduate will immediately go to combat units and deploy overseas. Many of you will threaten to kill yourselves to get out of real work, although you won't have the balls to actually do it!"

Brown's tone got softer as he attempted to clarify.

"Don't get me wrong here. Many of you will actually go fight and engage the enemy in close combat. For that I salute you. It takes a hard motherfucker to go kill people you've never met just because we say so."

The general then resumes his "motivational speech" to what he referred to as "the rest of you shit-stains."

"You'll most likely spend your deployment sitting on a FOB, manning guard towers, or waiting to go on patrols that get cancelled. I have a reality check for you all. Not everyone in this room is a hero. I don't give a shit what the beer commercials say. You drag your buddy out of a grape hut after you've stabbed two Taliban in the eyes with a broken MRE spoon then you're a motherfucking American Hero. You clear a trench with nothing but a sack of hand-grenades and your giant brass balls, then you're a motherfucking hero! But walking through the desert for three months without hearing a shot fired in anger and posting pictures in your combat gear doesn't make you a goddamned hero! I don't care what your family says. They're not heroes. Neither are your fucking wives. Hardest job in the Army, my ass! Damn it, I'm too old for this shit. Fuck you all."

Brown then threw up his middle finger to the crowd and stormed off the stage, hustling into his waiting staff car.

The silence after his speech was soon broken by wild applause from the assembled drill sergeants and officers responsible for training the young soldiers over the previous ten weeks.

Less enthusiasm was displayed by the families and the new graduates, who stormed the stage and attempted to destroy the auditorium to express their displeasure. The ensuing riot caused more than half a million dollars in damage, and drill sergeants were forced to kill 11 privates in self-defense.

An Army spokesman has said that Brown will not be scheduled as the keynote speaker for next week's graduation ceremony.

BEHIND THE BLOG

This may have been the first Duffel Blog article that made it on Snopes, the fact-checking site. Whenever we make Snopes, it is considered a high honor, since it means at least one person out there — perhaps your Uncle Bill — was forwarding around a Duffel Blog article with an all-caps comment of outrage. And then, Snopes, as it does, decides to debunk it.

Nowadays, making Snopes is pretty typical for popular articles. So, we've set our sights a little higher. Though we've successfully duped sitting U.S. Senators (more on that later), the top achievement for Duffel Blog now is to get a country to fall for an article.

Yeah, we're looking at you, China and North Korea.

Army Spends $100 Million On Piece Of Equipment That Doesn't Do Anything

By Sgt B

JOINT BASE LEWIS-MCCHORD, Wash. — After extensive research and development, the Army announced today that they would field a new piece of equipment that does absolutely nothing. The commander of 2nd Stryker Brigade, 2nd Infantry Division, was proud that his unit would be the first to acquire the new, high-quality, piece of shit.

"It's a great day for us here. The Army has spent over $50 million in R&D on this new thing that doesn't work at all and we're the first to have our soldiers not use it," said Col. Charles Winston. "The new piece of equipment, dubbed the M404, doesn't do anything at all and we couldn't be prouder to have it first to show the rest of the world how incapable this new thing is."

Sgt. Daniel Legget, a team leader in 1-17 INF, has already received several of the M404's and is tasked with evaluating how ineffective it is.

"This piece of shit — it doesn't do anything. It's great. Our unit has six of them. They weigh about 600lbs a piece so it's not easy to move around at all. We've taken them to the field four times already, and each time, they didn't do fucking anything," Legget said. "The M404 is the latest and greatest piece of shit that doesn't work in the Army, and I'm very proud that my team has been carrying them around for nothing."

Thomas Burns, an adviser to the Army who works for Xegis Solutions, had a hand in the M404's development.

"Gen. Odierno came to us and said, 'the Army needs something that's new and expensive. We've got about $80 million extra just lying around,'" said Burns. "I just went from there and made a large crate with no handles that weighs 650lbs. The inside is mostly concrete, and the outside is made out of slick teflon coating that's also considered stealth technology. That's where most of our budget went."

Burns believes the "low speed, high drag" piece of gear is exactly what the Army needs. "This thing, it doesn't really do shit, and it's almost impossible to find if you lose it. That's why we made it weigh so much. There's also no way to get a forklift under it. It's really a marvel of modern technology, and they only cost $5 million apiece."

Although many commanders have reacted with enthusiasm, feedback from soldiers who actually have to use the M404 has been mostly negative.

"What the fuck is this thing? It cost how much?" asked Spc. Joshua Bryant. "What the flying fuck is wrong with the Army? I can't even figure out a good way to lift this without at least 12 people."

Gen. Odierno testifies before Congress about the innovative and important piece of equipment Another soldier told Duffel Blog of an incident where the M404's stealth technology worked "extremely well".

"The other day we left one out in the field by mistake since we were in a hurry to get back," said Sgt. Frank Clinton. "We had the entire company on line doing a police call through the training area to find this stupid piece of fucking shit. The CO came out and said we weren't going home until we found it because it's considered a 'sensitive item'. What the fuck is sensitive about it? It doesn't do anything."

"I gotta go... we're still looking for it."

Gen. Odierno released a statement saying, "The Army plans to not use the M404 for ten years, and then hopefully sell it to the Marine Corps so it can continue to be useless."

At Naval Academy Graduation, Obama Lauds Future Scandal-Ridden, Sexual-Assaulting, Drunk Divorcées

By Juice Box

ANNAPOLIS, Md. — From a podium in the United States Naval Academy's storied Navy-Marine Corps Memorial Stadium, President Barack Obama offered hearty congratulations and a bit of advice to an exultant field of 1047 graduates about to take their first step into lives of substance abuse, scandal, and despair.

"Today – in this single, fleeting moment – we all are just so proud you," the president said in his commencement address. "Remember this, because it's probably all downhill from here."

Citing countless reports of adultery, alcoholism, rape, and dumbfounding incompetence discovered in the military's officer corps, Obama painted a candid picture of what the nation's best and brightest could look forward to upon entering the fleet as Navy ensigns and Marine Corps second lieutenants.

"Let's face it," the president told the expectant young officers. "The few of you that will be any good at your job at all will get out. The rest of you will be pushed through a broken promotion system that rewards mindless compliance with outdated standards over anything even vaguely resembling conscious human thought. As you rise through the ranks, you'll receive awards and honors you don't deserve and develop a wildly inflated sense of self, until finally you arrive in a position to grossly abuse the power and people in your charge. Give yourselves a round of applause."

The president went on to describe the great faith he put in the future leaders to renew public trust in military institutions but stated that they would likely fail miserably.

"As I look out at your bright, naïve faces, I see criminals on the cusp of realizing that none of this shit is anything like what you've seen in the movies. You all are in for crushingly early mornings and truly meaningless bureaucratic nonsense that will suck your soul dry. Life will suddenly seem very gray, and you'll probably start needing a drink just to get through the day."

"But still, a tip of my cap for the bang-up job you've done here at Annapolis."

The president was joined on stage by a number of senior military officials, including Secretary of the Navy Ray Mabus and Chief of Naval Operations Adm. Jonathan Greenert, who himself graduated from the Academy.

"Cherish these first years of your career," Mabus advised the midshipmen. "Work hard but don't forget to breathe in that fresh ocean air, because in the blink of an eye, twenty years will be gone and you'll find yourself on the front page of the Navy Times for fucking an enlisted person."

"Oh, and to the 80 percent of you fools who will be married in the next month, a heartfelt Mazel Tov," Mabus added. "Enjoy it while it lasts."

"Frankly, if last year's figures were any indication, an overwhelming number of you are headed for broken hearts and drawn-out custody battles – which makes sense when you consider the frequent deployments, dollar handjobs in Guam, and the fact that you've basically been prisoners on this campus for the last four years and have developed no social skills to speak of whatsoever."

After reciting the oath of office, amid cheers from family and friends, the proud disasters-to-be filed across the stage to receive their diplomas and shake hands with their Commander-in-Chief.

"I'd tell you not to disappoint us," Obama told one future naval aviator, "but at this point it's probably inevitable."

EOD Officer Getting His Ass Kicked By Intermediate Game Of Minesweeper

By Juice Box

ZABUL PROVINCE, AFGHANISTAN — In combat zones across the world, Navy Lt. Cmdr. Mike Kendall has rendered safe hundreds of live explosive devices, cheating death and saving countless lives in the process. Yet today sources confirm the decorated Explosive Ordinance Disposal officer is taking an outright beating from the popular computer game, Minesweeper.

"Son of a fucking... agh!" the expert bomb technician said, smacking his monitor and refreshing his game for the forty-third time this hour.

According to Kendall's colleagues at Special Operations Task Force Southeast, the trouncing began at approximately 9 o'clock this morning, when Kendall – reportedly emboldened by a successful game on Beginner yesterday – decided to try his hand at the Intermediate difficulty setting. Since then, it's been a non-stop pain train of "truly embarrassing" defeat for the man in a warfare community full of winners.

"The trick," Kendall said, squinting and rubbing bloodshot eyes, "is to learn the patterns. Right here, for instance, we've got a 1-2 pattern. That means this third tile over's always a mine, so now I just click – no, no, FUCK! Christ on Earth, where's a fucking robot when you need it?!" Indeed, Minesweeper challenges users like Kendall to logically determine where mines are hidden in a field of tiles based on hints which indicate the number of mines adjacent to any given tile; on the Intermediate level, 40 mines are hidden in a 16x16 tile field, making for one mine in every 6.4 tiles.

It's this simple but timeless code that right now is simply dismantling a man who actually knows how to take apart a nuclear bomb.

"Alright, listen up," Kendall barked to a watch floor of personnel tracking real and myriad explosive threats in the immediate vicinity of their forward operating base. "This crusty crab's got a score to settle. I'm gonna need a lunch and some adult diapers. Who are my volunteers?"

While members of Kendall's team say they admire the operator's persistence – and acknowledge a similar dedication to his work made Kendall the star in the EOD community he is – they really wish he would just win a goddamn game already or switch to a simpler diversion with less direct objectives, like Microsoft Paint.

"A man like that has absolutely nothing to prove," said one coworker found aimlessly wandering the camp. "And, to be honest, that's not even his fucking workstation."

For his part, Kendall says it's not about having anything to prove but about fostering a culture in the task force of tenacity and perseverance, no matter the odds. "In any case," he noted, "I'm pretty sure I've got this game that's come down to a fifty-fifty chance between two remaining tiles."

"Oh, HORSE SHIT," he added, just moments later.

At press time, hours had turned into days, and sources say the smell on the watch floor had grown unbearable. Meanwhile, an on-target SEAL platoon chief in Qalat city was concerned paths leading to a compound of interest might be rigged with IEDs.

"Goddamn," the chief said, checking his watch. "Why is EOD always so fucking late?!"

Pentagon Study Confirms: Napalm Does Stick To Kids

By G-Had

WASHINGTON, D.C. — An extremely controversial Pentagon study on the accuracy of various running and marching cadences has released its preliminary findings today, concluding that napalm does indeed stick to kids.

Col. Wallace Evans from the Army's Office of Motivation said the military had decided to conduct the study as part of an overall drive for more realism in training.

"We know the saying: train like you fight," said Evans. "So why are you going to be chanting something that you're never going to encounter in a combat environment?"

According to Evans, the drive to overhaul cadences came when after-action reports from the 75th Ranger Regiment on the popular multi-service "C-130 Rolling Down a Strip" cadence showed that not only did Airborne Rangers' chutes not open wide, but when the reserve failed they were not able to go after Satan.

"Most couldn't even penetrate the ground," according to Evans, "which raises a lot of questions of how they would get all the way down to Hell, assuming of course that Hell isn't an abstract concept ... but that was beyond the scope of this study."

The worst part, though, was when a group of soldiers visiting a Marine base in North Carolina heard the Marines claim that "C-130" was actually a Marine cadence.

"Everywhere on goddamn [Camp Lejeune] we kept hearing guys chanting about jumping out of airplanes," said Sergeant First Class Rafael Reyes. "I thought those fuckers were supposed to be amphibious."

The Office of Motivation then commissioned a several-year study to observe all popular cadences, as well as their accuracy. Even though "C-130" sparked the push for cadence reform, it was deemed too costly to use an entire regiment of Rangers as lawn darts.

"'Napalm' was actually our second choice for testing," Evans observed. "'Jesse James' seemed much more practical but most of our soldiers proved too heavy to ride a kangaroo, plus you can only kill so many long-haired hippies."

The popular "Napalm" cadence, which involves repeatedly chanting "Napalm sticks to kids," was created during the Vietnam War and has been reinforced in running cadences, jokes, and slogans. It is controversial, not only for its aggressive lyrics, but also from a multi-million-dollar lawsuit against the Army by the Dow Chemical Company over trademark infringement.

Early efforts to assess the cadence's accuracy raised more questions than they answered.

Popular rumors have attributed it to David Hackworth, but he claimed to his dying day that he'd first heard it in a Saigon whorehouse called The Pink Mist.

Unfortunately, despite the widespread use of the incendiary weapon, no conclusive testing had been done on the specific effects of the substance when used against targets under the age of eighteen.

"We tried coating the children in Teflon, butter, anything to make the napalm less sticky," said Capt. Alan Middleton, an Air Force liaison who took part in the napalm cadence testing, known informally as Operation Cooked Goose. "We even tried grease, although judging by the screams that didn't seem to help."

When pressed about a summary of the operation, Middleton smiled and replied, "After months of testing and hundreds of successfully engaged targets, we have conclusively determined that napalm does in fact stick to kids."

At press time, Col. Evans announced other studies underway to measure the temperature of female Eskimo genitalia, in addition to a nationwide search for an S&M Man to have sexual relations with your grandma on the front lawn as your grandfather cheers.

Duffel Blog reporters ArmyDave , ArmyJ, and Paul contributed to this report, and are surely going to hell for it.

BEHIND THE BLOG

This is one of my favorite stories because it is such a great way to figure out who "gets it." If you're a veteran, you've probably heard the cadence, so reading this story will make you laugh at how fucking dark we go.

But if you're not a veteran, it's likely you will be wondering what the fuck is wrong with the people who run Duffel Blog.

Interestingly enough, both of these reactions are right.

Budget Cuts Won't Reduce Massive Size Of First Cavalry Division Patch

By Maxx Butthurt

FORT HOOD, Texas — As conventional budget cuts loom on the heels of sequestration, leaders across the military are considering innovative and helpful ways to lower operating costs without hurting unit training or weapons qualifications.

However, one common-sense suggestion — "a no-brainer" according to one Pentagon official — has ruined at least one officer's career on the sprawling Army base of Fort Hood.

The suggestion: Shrink the enormous 1st Cavalry Division patch down to a size comparable to the rest of the military.

The storied division has seen action in every American conflict since its 1921 formation. The most notable thing about the unit is not their impressive combat record, though, but their patch: an elephantine black and yellow Norman shield sporting a horse head.

Unlike other military emblems, the 1st Cav insignia has been known actually to extend below the elbows of shorter soldiers, and is greeted with a level of mockery and derision usually reserved for things like the green fleece cap, or ACUs.

Miles Detrich, a discharged Army captain and former comptroller for the 2nd Brigade of the 1st Cav, was the man who ignited the firestorm. Duffel Blog talked to the now-unemployed Detrich while he sat drinking at a dirty bar in Killeen, Texas.

"It all seemed so simple you know? Our Colonel told us budget cuts were coming, and we'd have to get creative with how the units spent money. Everyone else was coming up with off-the-wall stuff, while this was staring us right in the face. Literally," said Detrich sighing and gesturing at his own worn 1st Cav patch, which he had removed to hang on the back of his chair, dangling and brushing the floor.

"Did you know these things cost the Army over fifty bucks a piece? Look at it. Fifty fucking bucks! Ridiculous!"

Shortly after formalizing the suggestion to reduce the size of the patch by a mere two inches, Detrich was given a General Letter of Reprimand by his chain of command and removed from the company commander's list. Less than two weeks later he was presented with his paperwork and chaptered out of the Army, three years before his scheduled ETS date. Now, Mr. Detrich sits, alone and jobless, wishing his impressive resume lands him a job offer, but he's not hopeful.

"After my little incident, no one in this town will even look at me. I can't even move away. My entire family is from this area. I can't even get a job flipping burgers after my commander followed through on his threat to make sure I'd never work again."

The man glanced around the empty bar and finished his beer in one long gulp, the very embodiment of self-loathing. "All I wanted to do was save the Army some money. Was that so wrong?"

According to Division Command Sgt. Maj. James Norman, the answer is an emphatic yes.

"This punk-ass captain is going to come along and say we need to change the damn patch? Almost a century of blood and tradition behind those colors, and some paper-pushing finance weenie decides to save a few nickels by shitting on the legacy of countless better men before him," said Norman, who became increasingly annoyed.

"Well, not on my watch! We've got plenty of money. I don't understand what those queers up in Washington do all day, but I know the Army will always have cash to spend. In fact, just this week I commissioned a gold-plated statue of the patch to be placed in front of the headquarters building, just to remind all our young troopers that they're part of the First Team! HOOAH?"

He smiled as if envisioning the future memorial.

"We've also got a plan in the works to extend the size of the combat patch by another 2 inches, and add diamond studs to the spurs that we veterans have the privilege of wearing at every social function, on-post and off!"

When the sergeant major finished, he was shown several documents.

The first was a report that highlighted the fact that not only was Detrich's proposal to trim the 1st Cav patch sound financial advice, it would have saved the Army enough money to deploy an entire combat brigade to and from Afghanistan, twice. The second was an excerpt from Capt. Detrich's service record showing he was actually a decorated infantry officer who'd earned the Silver Star medal before being forced into the comptroller position.

Norman refused to back down, calling Detrich a "fucking POG," before breaking into a horribly off-key version of Garryowen, the 1st Cavalry Division song, and ending the interview.

Hooah? Hooah!

By Armydave

HOOAH, HH – Hooah hooah hoaohhoah hoah. Hooah hooahhooah hooahhooahhoah hoah, hooah hooah hooah hooah. Hooah hoah hoah hoah hoah hooah. Hoahhooahhooah hoah hooah hoah hoah. Hoah hooah ho-ah.
HOOAAAHHH!!

"Hooah," hoah Hooah. "Hooooooooahhhhhhhh."

Hooahhooah hoah hooah hoah. Hoah hooah hoahhoahhoah hoah hoah. Hoahhoah Hoahhoah Hoahhoah (HOAH) hooah. Hoahhoah hoah hoah, hoah hoah hoah hoah, hoah hoah hoah. Hoah hoah hoah hoah hoah. Hooah hoah hoahhoah hoah hoah hoah — hoahhoahohoah. Hoah hoahhoahhoah hoah. Hoahhoah hoah hoah hoah hoahoahhoahhoahhoah. Hoah hoah hoah hoah hoah hoah hoah hoah. Hooahhoah hoahhoah hoahhoah hooahhoahhoahhoah. Hooah hoah hoah hoah; hoah hoah hoahhoah. Hooah hoah hoah.

"Hoah hoah hooahhoah?" Hoah hoah hoah.

"Hoah hoah, hoah hooahhoah hoah," Hoah hooah. "Hoah hoah hooahhoah."

Hooah Hooah.

Hoahhoah hooah hoah hoah. HOAH Hoah hoah hoahhoahhoah hoah hoah. Hoahhoah Hoahhoah hoah. Hoahhoah hoah hoah, hoah hoah hoah hoah, hoah hoah hoah. Hooah hoah hoah hoah -- hoahhoahhoah. Hoah hoahhoahhoah hoah. Hoahhoah hoah hoah hoah. Hoahoah hoahhoah hoah. Hoah hoah hoah hoah hoah hoah hoah hoah. Hoahhoah hoahhoah hoahhoah hoahhoahhoahhoah. Hoah hoah hoah hoah; hoah hoah hoahhoah. Hoah hoah hoah. Hoah hoah hoahhoah hoah.

Hoah HOAH Hoah Hoah hoah hoah, "Hoahhoah hoahhoah hoah."

"Hooooooahhhh!!!" Hoah hoah hoahhoah hoah hoah hoah hoahhoahhoah. Hoah hooahhoahhoah hoah. Hoahhoah hoah hoah hoah hoahoahhoahhoahhoah. Hoah hoah hoah hoah hoah hoah hoah hoah. Hoahhoah hoahohoah hoahhoah hoahhoahhoahhoah. "Hoah hoah hoah hoah hoah" hoah hoahhoah. Hoah hoah hoah. Hoah hoah hoahhoah hoah hoah hooah hoahhoahhoah. Hoah hoahhoahhoah hoah. Hoahhoah hoah hoah hoah hoahoah; hoahhoahhoah hoah. Hoah hoah hoah hoah hoah hoah hoah hoah. Hoahhoah hoahhoah hoahhoah hoahhoahhoahhoah. Hoah hoah hoah hoah; hoah hoah hoahhoah. Hoah hoah hoah. Hoah hoahhoahhoah hoah. Hoahhoah hoah hoah hoah hoahoahhoahhoahhoah. Hoah hoah hoah hoah. Hoah hoah hoah hoah hoah
Hooah, HOOOAHH!
hoah hoah hoah. Hoahhoah HOAH hoahhooah hoahhoah hoahhoahhoahhooah. Hoah hoah hoah hoah; hoah hoah hoahhoah. Hoah hoah hoah. hooah hoah hoah hoah. Hoahhoah hoahhoah hoahhoah hoahhoahhoahhoah. Hoah hoah hoah hoah; hoah hoah hoahhoah. Hoah HOAH hooahhoahhoah hoah. Hoahhoah hoah hoah hooah hoahoahhoahhoahhoah.

"Hoah hoah hooah, hoahhoahhoah." Hoah hoah.

Hoah hoah hoahhooah hoah hoah hoah -- hoahhoah hoah. Hoah hoahhoahhoah hoah. Hoahhoah hoah hoah hoah hoahoahhoahhoahhoah. Hooah hoah hoah hoah hoah hoah hoah hoah. Hoahhoah hoahhoah hoahhoah hoahhooahhoahhoah. Hoah hoah hoah hoah; hoah hoah hoahhoah. Hooah hoah hoah."

"HOOAH!"

BEHIND THE BLOG

I'm a Marine, so when I first read this article by Armydave, I had no fucking idea what I was looking at.

I honestly still don't know what I'm looking at, but I trusted that Dave knew what the hell he was doing and I published it anyway.

As it turns out, a ton of soldiers loved this article and shared it like crazy. So, hooah.

Marine Still Trying To Craft Perfect Signature Block After Promotion To Staff Sergeant

By Paul Sharpe

CAMP PENDLETON, Calif. — A Marine staff sergeant with 1st Battalion, 4th Marines motor transport is desperately trying to put the finishing touches on his email signature block, officials confirmed.

Staff Sgt. Jason Winters, 33, who was promoted to his present rank on May 1, is not sure whether to use a motivational quote from a legendary Medal of Honor recipient, a major historical figure, or his lieutenant.

Winters is not alone in his signature block frustration. In accordance with Marine Corps regulations, every staff non-commissioned officer is required to place a signature block at the end of their email, requiring a minimum of 750 words.

"They need to have a sign-off, such as 'Regards' or 'Very Respectfully', their name, rank, date of birth, and other pertinent information, and then a closing quote," said Capt. Randy Schuster, a Marine spokesman in Quantico, Virginia.

"I'm just not sure about this," said a distraught Winters as he looked over a variety of quotes from Chesty Puller and Dan Daly. "Sure, I could use a quote from Chesty, but the sergeant major uses one of those and he might get upset."

Winters can't decide whether he should go with "Come on you sons of bitches! Do you want to live forever?" from Daly, or "We're surrounded, that simplifies the problem," from Puller.

"I could go with the obvious Dan Daly quote, but what if I email some infantry sergeant with that at the end?" asked Winters. "I mean, sure I've been on convoys in Iraq so I'm practically a rifleman anyway, but I don't want people to think I'm just some dumb pogue."

"Maybe I'll go with a Bible verse," Winters added. "I kind of like 'I am become death. The destroyer of worlds.'"

While Winters runs through potential quotes that he is sure "will motivate the young devil dogs that read it," he also needs to worry about the "little things" that he says make the perfect email sign-off.

"Should I close with Very Respectfully, or just V/R?" Winters mused. "Or do I go really bold? Maybe put 'Semper Fidelis,' or 'Whatever it Takes!' — our battalion motto."

The new staff sergeant also needs to decide what else to place below V/R — the sign-off he's currently leaning towards. Friends in the motor pool told Duffel Blog reporters that he was thinking of putting his rank, name, radio call-sign ("Hondo Hardcore"), email address, office telephone number, mobile number, Iraq and Afghanistan deployment numbers, other units he's served with, PFT score, and other "vital information needed at the end of every email sent."

"Unfortunately, the email software doesn't allow Marines to just double-click on my name and see what unit I'm with and see my phone number," said Winters. "And since I'm sending an email from my usmc.mil address, they also can't just hit reply and get back to me. They need to see that in my signature block."

At press time, desperation overcame Winters as he added up the words for his email signature — bringing it under the regulation requirement at a measly 647 words.

"I think I'm going to have to just bite the bullet on this one and take from someone else," said Winters, as he copy-and-pasted an obscure confidentiality agreement below the signature block that gives the impression he's either in the CIA or a complete asshole.

BEHIND THE BLOG

Is there anything worse than the person who emails you and has, in his signature block, an inspirational quote from himself? That's not bullshit. I've actually gotten that email.

I don't know what it is about signature blocks in the military, but everyone seems to think they need to have all kinds of crazy information. Phone numbers, emails (why? I can just hit fucking reply), quotes, unit logos, privacy act statements, and their blood type.

Still, I wrote this article to make fun of those people with dumb signature blocks, and yet I'm going to self-report here as a one-time offender who likely had too much stuff down there. But I still never used a quote from myself.

As a service to readers, I'm going to supply you with a handy cut-and-paste signature block below:

Rank and Name
Unit
DSN:
"I hate you all." —Paul Szoldra, founder of Duffel Blog

American Suicide Bombers Attack Taliban Office In Qatar

By Courtney Massengale

DOHA, QATAR — The recently opened office of the Taliban has come under attack by American insurgents, sources confirmed Tuesday.

The complex attack on the facility included a vehicle-borne IED from a Ford F-150, gunmen armed with AR-15s, and Chili's Baby Back Ribs lobbed from outside the compound's perimeter.

"I never saw anything like it. Well, at least not from the receiving end," said Abbud Abdul-Basit, a Taliban fighter who witnessed the attack. "They just charged the gate like they didn't care! I mean, that was effective. I always wondered why it worked so well."

"They were chanting 'USA! USA!' and 'Git R Done.' I close my eyes and I can still hear them," said Tariq Uthman, a guard from Khyber Pakhtunkhwa. "I can't tell my wife, or my friends back home. How can they understand such utter senselessness?"

A Taliban spokesman said there was no reason to believe the attackers were citizens of Qatar.

"All evidence points to the attack being conducted by foreign fighters from America," said Taliban spokesman Zabiullah Mujahid. "We have recovered literature from an American extremist organization, the NRA, from the truck. The deceased fighters were wearing Under Armour shirts and Oakley glasses. We also believe they may have received training at CrossFit training camps in North Carolina."

Jay Carney, a spokesman for the Americans, stated that the government of the United States had no connection to the attacks and did not condone violence in the struggle to bring the 21st century to the Middle East.

"We are a peace-loving people, but when the greatest tenets of western civilization are mocked, we cannot control what true believers of 'Murica may do," Carney said. "They have died heroes and may their bodies be returned to small towns in the Midwest and rural south with 72 Patriot Guards riding beside them."

Reaction in the Taliban stronghold of Waziristan, Pakistan was swift and somber.

"Who are these cowards who disguise themselves as civilians and blow up women and children just to oooohhhhhhhhh....." said resident Abdul Rackman Muhammad. "Um, maybe I should rethink some things. Yeah, totally not as cool when it's happening to you."

The Taliban established its office in Qatar to enter negotiations with the United States and the government of Afghanistan. Mujahid insisted the recent attack has not derailed these delicate talks.

"This does nothing to change our goal of imposing Sharia Law throughout the region and reverting Afghanistan to the stone age. If the Americans think one attack will stop us and our tribal partners from banging goats and beating women, they are sadly mistaken."

Up-Armored Golf Carts Arrive At Bagram Country Club

By Frederick Taub

BAGRAM AIR FORCE BASE, AFGHANISTAN — The first shipment of reinforced golf carts has arrived in theater at Bagram Air Force Base near the Afghan capital of Kabul, sources reported today.

"The new G-01F Enhanced Personnel Transporter is the latest addition to our warfighting capabilities here on the ground," said Brig. Gen. Daniel Kosciuszko, Commander of Air Lift Wing 13, in a press conference. "Initially, I got some serious push-back from [former CENTCOM Commander] Gen. Mattis on the subject. He called me a [expletive deleted] candyass fairy Air Force [expletive deleted] Polack and bodily threw me out of his office."

Koscuiszko paused to bring up a picture of the improved equipment on his slide show.

"Fortunately, Gen. Allen was so busy with the impending catastrophic defeat of his forces in Kandahar that I was able to slip this request by his G4," he said.

Fielding a question from the Duffel Blog about the military purpose behind the glorified golf cart, Kosciuszko defended his position with panache.

"Look here. The Army and the Marines are always going on about not having adequate protection for their men out in the field. What about the lives of my airmen? Are they somehow less valuable just because they're on the golf course and not clearing routes of IEDs? I'll have you know that 33% of my Wing's emergency room visits have been sustained while out on the links, and I will be damned if I have to write another letter home to a loved one about an injury that could have been prevented by our new up-armored carts."

"Besides," Kosciuszko added, "Now we finally have something to do with those completely impractical MRAPs that doesn't involve selling them to incompetent third-world countries or sending them straight to the junk yards to get scrapped."

The Air Force Chief of Staff agreed.

"The G-01F?" said Gen. Mark A. Welsh III. "Oh, it's great stuff! Great stuff! I personally testified before Congress about its usefulness to the war effort. Not only is its manufactured in no less than 30 states, but the main assembly factory for this baby is located in Ithaca, New York! Boy did that score points with [Secretary of the Army] McHugh!"

Welsh also noted what he called "the finest in Air Force safety features."

"It comes combat-ready with two five-point harnesses, a roll cage, airbags, and extra reflective bumpers," said Welsh, who went on to say that regrettably — despite the service's best efforts — an initiative to install ejection seats was rejected by risk management officials as being 'too impractical.'

At press time, three airmen had been killed and one critically injured in a rollover incident involving their G-01F between Holes 11 and 12.

USMC To Deploy Alabamian Code Talkers

By Erik Sullivan

FORT MCCLELLAN, Ala. – The United States Marine Corps is poised to resurrect its legendary Code Talker Program by attaching several native Alabamians to Marine infantry units currently deployed to Afghanistan, sources confirmed.

"Ahm jus' tickled as a dern coon in ah 'shine bucket!" hooted Pfc. Bobby Joe Carson. "Bout to hitch ah scoot ta that there whachacallit Ganderstan an hand out a hidin' ta thems Towelie-bans."

Made famous in the Pacific Theater of World War II, the original Code Talkers used the Navajo language as a form of encrypted communication during a number of critical engagements. The use of Navajo was an exercise in wartime ingenuity that kept the Japanese guessing and saved countless American lives. With so many of America's modern enemies taking the time to learn English, the call was again sounded for American citizens who speak their own indecipherable dialects.

"Cain't never coulda seent this kinda catawampus 'bout the way I talked ma words out," Carson marveled. "Used ta be them Yankee fancy talkers'd get madder'n a wet hen 'bout the way I talked and that'd just dill my pickle sumthin' fierce."

Military Intelligence specialists have worked for several months with a handful of America's most incomprehensible citizens to ensure their smooth integration into the Marine Corps. They have also undertaken the laborious task of training specialized linguists to decipher the new Code Talker transmissions.

The program has overcome a series of serious hurdles, including complaints from equal opportunity offices over the Code Talkers' frequent utilization of homophobic slurs and the N-word.

"Who are we to impose our cultural norms on these proud people?" Maj. William Thompson, the Intelligence Liaison for the Code Talkers, said in response to the criticism. "If their only way to describe the night sky is 'negro freckles,' who are we to judge 200 years of social evolution?"

Further complications arose early in the program when officers realized that the Code Talkers simply did not have words for mission-critical vocabulary such as "GPS," "computer" or "integration." Fortunately, once the terms were explained, dialectic equivalencies were generated, which resulted in "Spaceship maps," "boring televisions" and "the devil's work," respectively.

"I'm plumb si-gogglin' rightch yonder dem goldern peckerwood airish in tha poke oh flower wit them wharf rats," asserted Carson. "Roll Tide!"

You Know What? Screw It, Everyone's Gonna Wear Three Reflective Belts At All Times

By Paul Sharpe

The following is an opinion piece by Sergeant Major of the Army Raymond F. Chandler III.

You know what soldiers? I'm sick and tired of this crap.

You want to keep complaining about having to wear reflective belts? You don't like that you have to wear the thing in Afghanistan in the middle of a combat zone? It's not 'cool' to have to put that on your uniform, you say. Well, you know what? Screw it. Everyone's going to wear three of the flippin' things at all times.

Yeah, you heard me. Three.

Goddamn it, these things are saving your worthless little lives.

Oh, how are you supposed to wear three reflective belts, you ask. Well, first off, I'm a sergeant major, so I don't need to answer any of your questions. Second, how about you figure that stuff out yourselves? You can adapt on the battlefield, now you need to adapt with a reflective piece of plastic that keeps you from getting flattened like a goddamn pancake when a Humvee rolls by.

Don't think it could happen? Think again.

Bagram Air Field, 2004. Soldiers just walking around, lollygagging, thinking they're back on the block. BOOM. No reflective belt. Dead. Saw it happen, it was terrible. But you know what, with his last dying breath, that soldier told me, "Sergeant Major, if only I had been wearing my reflective belt, I would be alive. Please tell my mother I—, no, tell the other soldiers they need to be safe with reflective belts on at all times."

Well, I'm granting that dying wish right now. You troops are going to wear your reflective belts everywhere. I don't care whether you are doing PT, in your dress uniform, or out at the bar drinking and trying to score some late-night action, you're going to have "three of your PPE" [personal protective equipment] around your bodies at all times.

Ok, good, you want to keep complaining?

We're wearing four of the goddamn things. I can go all day, soldiers. Don't push me. If they can't see our 0500 PT formation from the flipping space station, that's a no-go. Hooah?

If I keep hearing complaints or seeing any more bull crap about how you don't like your reflective belt — so help me. If you like the Multicam uniform, you just wait until me and the general testify before congress for the new and improved Multireflect uniform.

Don't make me do it, soldiers.

Right now, go grab your reflective belts, and put them on. You'll thank me later.

You heard me. Five of them.

Navy Chief Indoctrination Culminates In Human Sacrifice

By Epic Blunder

WORLDWIDE – Doomsday prophecies were actualized in an unholy and gruesome ceremony as the United States Navy inducted its freshest batch of minions into the Chief's Mess, sources confirmed Friday.

Awestruck commands worldwide stood paralyzed with fear as each Chief Petty Officer selectee for fiscal year 2013 opened his or her mysterious wooden box, consuming the souls of the countless sailors they had drained during their years of service. The lacquered boxes, affixed with each Selectee's name and warfare designation, have been on their person since board results were announced six weeks ago.

"I always wondered what the deal with those boxes was," shrugged Petty Officer 2nd Class Dan Patterson.

Typical of naval ceremonies, each Chief Petty Officer frocking ceremony commenced with close-order drill and "Anchors Aweigh." Unbeknownst to wardroom and crew alike, the very order and nature of the ceremonies called upon Moloch [the pagan deity] and other foul, demonic specters, beckoning forth darkened skies, howling winds and a rain of unholy fire.

Command Master Chiefs lay prostrate before a communal coffee mug, uttering words of a long-forgotten tongue before offering the consecrated grounds to each Selectee.

"Take this, all of you, and drink from it. For this is full-bodied, and way better than that shit on the mess decks."

Each Selectee was then prompted to open their box, unleashing the tormented wails of over-managed and overworked sailors of commands-past. As the selectees absorbed each soul and their eyes grew with a ravenous thirst for power, witnesses proclaimed to have seen their waistbands expand threefold, transforming each selectee into a fearsome, khaki silhouette bereft of jawline and reasonable thought.

Ceremonies concluded with the customary human sacrifice of hurling an unassuming victim under a bus driven by the Command Master Chief. Although some commands elected to forego tradition and offered sacrifice by forcibly sodomizing their victims to death, all rituals were universal in the drowning of the victims' screams for mercy by the shrill cry of the boatswain's pipe and the words, "Chief Petty Officer, United States Navy, arriving."

Female Marine Charges Obstacle Course With Sexual Harassment

By Nick Shafer

OKINAWA, JAPAN – Charges of sexual harassment have been brought against the base obstacle course this week, after a female Marine from 7th Communications Battalion reported that "she felt extremely uncomfortable doing physical training on or around the object."

The Marine, who wishds to remain anonymous, claims the O-course behaved in an inappropriate manner during a unit physical training session.

"I have never felt so ashamed and violated in my life. The course was all over my lady parts, then, it [the o-course] made me do terrible things," she said.

Soon after the female Marine's meritorious promotion to corporal, her battalion commander released a statement.

"I currently have an investigation underway, but right now, we are concerned for this Marine's welfare," said Lt. Col. Nicholas J. Lourian. "I will order a Battalion safety stand-down as soon as we have some answers so that this incident doesn't happen again."

This isn't the first case at Camp Hansen. Some female Marines have complained about the abbreviation for portable radio component (PRC), which is pronounced "prick" by many male Marines. Others say they've endured a barrage of sexual harassment at the enlisted club, with male Marines "inappropriately buying them drinks."

"Even at the PX I'm getting treated like a piece of meat," said one female Marine who spoke on condition of anonymity. "Sometimes when I get in line, there will be a couple of men ahead, saying that I can cut them and go ahead, trying to act nice. I may be a woman but I have every right to stand in the PX line just like the men."

Most male Marines were unsure of how to take the news.

"This is bullshit! Do you know how long it takes me to get anything done so I don't hurt anyone's overly-sensitive feelings?" said Sgt. James Simpson. "I am calling my monitor and getting out of this shit sandwich."

Marine Commandant Gen. James Mattis ignored repeated requests for interview on the matter, but after considerable pressure, sent a fax to Duffel Blog which only read:

"Harden The Fuck Up.

Very Respectfully Submitted with Titty Sprinkles,

M-4"

Lt. Col. Lourian reports that his emergency ethics stand-down for the battalion has been a great success.

"Sgt. Simpson gave multiple classes on professionalism, suicide prevention, and sexual harassment — which were really great and I think helped the Marines quite a bit."

According to witnesses at the brief, Lourian sat quietly behind his Battalion, stroking and whispering to a set of colonel insignia that he keeps in his cover.

Pentagon Channel Celebrates 100th Viewer

By Ron

FORT MEADE, Md. — All three employees of the Pentagon Channel attended a lunch yesterday to celebrate a major milestone in the network's history.

This week's Nielsen ratings reported that two separate viewers tuned in to TPC last week, pushing the total number of people who have ever watched the channel to 100.

The celebration lunch was held at a reserved table at CiCi's Pizza, located in the 6400 block of Baltimore National Pike in Baltimore.

"I try not to get caught up in things like 'ratings' or 'popularity,'" said Chester Perkins, TPC's General Manager. "This was a big deal, though, and I wanted to commemorate it. It's just nice to get together for a hot lunch."

Perkins has been an employee of the Defense Media Activity and its predecessor, the American Forces Information Services, since 1958. He has been in charge of TPC since it went on the air in 2004.

"Old Chet [Perkins] has been, to put it politely, resistant to change," said Mike Carey, TPC Director of Programming. "The History Channel pulls great numbers with its war documentaries, and there are plenty of popular military-themed movies and shows out there. I keep pitching ideas for programs that people might actually want to watch, but Chet says that's not what we're about here."

One of Carey's ideas that did make it was Close Combat, which broke down combatives techniques from all four services and showed fights from a 2010 military-wide combatives tournament. The martial arts-themed subject matter generated some initial interest, but failed to attract even a single viewer.

"Close Combat was a quality program and I wanted it on in primetime, but Chet insisted that we bury it in a Saturday morning time slot," Carey said. "He made us fill the primetime hours with some kind of Army talent show that literally no one watched."

Perkins said he doesn't use ratings to determine programming, but instead trusts his instincts.

"Good folks nowadays don't want to watch shows that are entertaining or fun," Perkins said. "They want to watch NCOs grilling outside on a warm summer afternoon, or young troops playing video games and riding go-karts, or news about change of command ceremonies and the Combined Federal Campaign."

"They want tours of military installations," Perkins added, "and to watch soldiers doing PT, and low-budget military documentaries produced by military public affairs offices in the 1960s." Perkins crossed his arms proudly and leaned back in his chair. "I've been saying all that for years, and judging from the latest ratings, turns out I was right. We had two viewers last week. I try not to let it get to my head, but sometimes you gotta just pat yourself on the back."

The lunch ended when a third member of the group, studio technician Leroy Bradley, had to leave so that he could be back at his desk in time for a job interview over the phone with the Golf Channel.

Pentagon Proposes Controversial Policy Assigning Ranks To Military Spouses

By John "Whiskey Tango Foxtrot" Mittle

FAYETTEVILLE, N.C. — A new policy is currently being considered by the Department of Defense which would assign rank to spouses of military members.

The controversial measure which was announced yesterday is meant to address disputes and complaints. Problems would be handled between spouses instead of a dependents' chain of command.

With a system of rank would also come legal doctrine — The Civilian Code of Spousal Justice — to mirror the military's existing Uniform Code of Military Justice.

The policy discussion comes after a high-profile incident in which a Marine wife was not saluted as she entered her husband's base, as well as a series of surveys conducted throughout the military to determine major issues plaguing the force. Many commanders described frustrating encounters with military spouses on "an almost daily basis."

Some of the survey findings were startling, showing commanders finding it increasingly difficult to mediate issues between military spouses. With troop drawdowns and lack of manpower, polls show a force dealing with problems on the home front even more than military combat.

One survey returned from a Marine platoon commander at Camp Pendleton expressed anger at what he called "dependopotamouses."

"I can't handle this anymore. I'm supposed to be a Sniper Platoon Commander, not some lovey dovey, let's be friends, kumbaya, sit around the camp-fire playing acoustic guitar freak," said 1st Lt. Nathan Morris. "Shit, no wonder my Scout Snipers are out of control. Their spouses drive them insane."

A company commander with the Army's 25th Infantry Division told a similar story.

"No shit, there I was, surrounded on all fronts. There had to be at least 25 of em','" recalled Capt. Eric Jones. "Hollering their war cries of demands for higher BAH and less field time for their husbands."

After establishing a focus group of 20 field grade officers, the idea of assigning military spouses' rank was brought up by Maj. Alex Steen.

"This is a wonderful idea," Steen said. "Many spouses already seem to act like they wear their sponsors' rank, so why not just give it to them? This will allow spouses to pull rank when necessary so as to put out-of-line spouses in their respective place."

The DoD has proposed ranks be assigned to dependents of sponsors in pay-grades of E-1 through E-9. The spousal rank would also be equivalent to the sponsors' rank to avoid instances of "pulling rank" on the military sponsor.

Spouse ranks would begin with S-1 (Spouse Recruit) and ascend to S-9 (Chief Master Spouse).

"If only this had been done sooner," said Ellen Trump, wife of Sgt. Maj. John Trump. "One time I was sitting outside of the PX when this — this Lance Corporal's wife, tattoo sleeves and all, walks by with her two kids. Doesn't stop. Doesn't give the proper greeting of the day. I've been married to the Marine Corps for over 20 years! I think she needs to learn who her betters are!"

The new Civilian Code of Spousal Justice will include Articles pertaining to insubordination, assaulting or willfully disobeying superior ranked spouses, and malingering so as to grant authority to the prospective ranks.

The Pentagon has not yet confirmed or denied the possibility of assigning rank to the spouses of officers.

BEHIND THE BLOG

This was one of those articles which turned into a gigantic shitshow. And by shitshow, I mean total hilarity on our end. But you can be damn sure that letters to the editor were written in base newspapers, and social media was on fire about the controversial new policy of assigning ranks to spouses.

I can't think of any other profession where a spouse identifies themselves as part of their partner's profession. There's no such thing as a Supermarket Manager wife, or a Marketing husband. And yet, the military wife or husband is a thing.

To be fair, I've met plenty of military spouses who don't take themselves too seriously.

But there are plenty more who think they have pull in the PX based on their spouses' rank. Remember: The question of "do you know who my husband is?" should always get a response of a sarcastic "thank you for your service."

US, China Agree To Hate Each Other As Friends

By Dark Laughter

RANCHO MIRAGE, Calif. — Following joint U.S.-China talks Friday, Presidents Barack Obama and Xi Jinping released a new joint declaration of principles that stated the two countries had agreed that they were in total disagreement on basically all issues of governance, had essentially no common interests in spite of being economically intertwined, and would continue to attempt to undermine each other at every turn by any means necessary.

However, it also stated that the leaders had agreed that this rivalry to the death would not impact the two countries' fundamental good relations, and that China and the United States hoped to continue to enjoy each other's friendship while attempting to destroy one another.

Speaking to the press afterwards about what prompted the decision, the two stated that the breakthrough came while talking about North Korea.

"I was pressing him about China's backing of North Korea," said Obama, "and we were both feeling very frustrated. Finally, he said 'stop asking me for things you know I can't give you. You know the situation. Our support for North Korea is just geopolitics ... we hate those crazy, embarrassing assholes and they hate us right back. It's like the opposite of our relationship with you.'"

"I asked him what he meant, and he said that even though China is a direct and active rival of the U.S. that wants to see us crumble in the long term, they still view the United States with great affection and respect," he added.

"That was when we had our breakthrough, because it dawned on me that's exactly how Americans think of China as well. We're like the Smiths and the Joneses — two basically good neighbors who are in friendly competition that won't end until one of them is dead and the other is crying on their grave, probably while also pissing on it."

"When China looks at the United States, we're amazed at how similar our people are," said Xi. "Generous, optimistic, hard-working, xenophobic, envious, and arrogant. When we compare your pluralist plutocracy to ours, we sometimes think the only way it could be better is if you were Chinese as well."

Under the terms of the agreement, China will continue to conduct cyberattacks on U.S. businesses and government agencies, but the U.S. will initiate similar attacks on the personal computers of Chinese officials in search of evidence of corruption, which they will then leak to the Chinese public. Both countries agreed to deny all knowledge of these activities when discovered in order to prevent awkwardness that might impact their friendship.

Regarding the theft of advanced military designs, Obama said he was willing to overlook it in the interest of moving forward diplomatically.

"Let's be honest," he said, "They are stealing plans for the F-35 and the Expeditionary Fighting Vehicle. China would do more damage to itself by building them than any of these vehicles would ever do to us on the battlefield."

With the resolution on cyberattacks, the two were able to subsequently achieve a stunning string of additional agreements, such as on economics, climate change, and security.

"It is agreed that we will continue to buy up U.S. debt to artificially weaken our currency and encourage trade," said Xi, "but we will no longer attempt to scare our friends in America by pretending that there is any way to use this as leverage to attain military objectives without also destroying the economy of China."

"For our part, we will continue to allow your currency manipulation," said Obama, "and we will no longer talk about finding ways to coerce you into complying with climate change initiatives. Instead, we will continue to sell you coal to fuel your ongoing cancer epidemic, and we will continue to subject your imports to transparent consumer protection standards, then release the shocking results to your people via the internet."

"It is agreed that the United States will continue to meddle in the affairs of China's neighbors, to include propping up the Province of Taiwan," said Xi. "We hope you have no problems with sexual assaults by your troops in Japan, Australia, and Vietnam. We will happily postpone our inevitable hegemony in Southeast Asia while waiting on the United States to alienate allies through off base incidents and eventually run out of money for foreign adventures. We can use that time to focus on developing our influence in the west."

"On behalf of the American people, we wish you the best of luck there, and hope that your Hui Muslim population makes many new friends," chuckled Obama.

When asked for more details about what this new declaration would mean for the military and intelligence communities, the two leaders pledged greater cooperation.

"We talked about it, and we'd like to see our militaries train together more often. We can both agree that we want stability, so we need to ensure that we have buy-in from these potentially destabilizing and more belligerent factions," said Obama.

"Joint training is a simple solution," offered Xi. "These higher-level commanders like getting plaques and medals that provide them with legitimacy, and joint training is the best way to do that without sending them to war. Also, joint training would be an excellent opportunity for our intelligence services to recruit assets and steal sensitive data."

"Not to mention a great chance to expose Chinese intelligence personnel to American freedoms, and get them to start thinking about how to betray their bosses and jump ship to go live in Canada or Australia when China finally implodes," added Obama.

The two then shook hands, and left to play another round of golf before the night's pig roast, laughing like old friends.

Can Of Dip Miraculously Lasts Eight Days In The Field

By Donnell

FORT DRUM, N.Y. — A battered can of Copenhagen dip lasted eight whole days in the field with the 10th Mountain Division, Army sources confirm. This miracle occurred during a field exercise with the 2-87 Catamount Battalion.

Battalion leadership conducted a last-minute shakedown before heading out to the field, defiling tobacco stockpiles in accordance with a new morale-crushing policy just before jump off.

"Tobacco kills my soldiers," Sgt. Maj. James Burton explained. "So do toxic marriages and traumatic brain injuries, but we can't ban tits and IEDs now can we?"

The first night in the field, Spc. Judah Berkowitz, an infantryman from Queens, New York, made an amazing discovery.

"I was digging a fighting position," said Berkowitz. "See? Right here, I made it out of clay. And when it was dry and ready I hopped in and found a half-buried can of Copenhagen."

The tobacco lasted for eight days, against all odds. "I still can't believe it," platoon mooch Pfc. John Peters said. "That can never ran out. I must've bummed a dozen pinches from that chump and I didn't put a dent in it. Hey, can I grab a Marlboro while we're talking?"

Berkowitz and his dip inspired the unit to greatness during the exercise, and the soldier received a challenge coin for his leadership. Burton melted chocolate onto the coin first, however, because he "heard your people do that around this time of year."

The Catamount battalion has dubbed Berkowitz's story the "Miracle of Hannu-Cope."

U.S. Military Divorcing Afghanistan For Hotter, Sexier War

By G-Had

KABUL, AFGHANISTAN – The United States Military and Afghanistan will be getting a divorce after eleven years of war so the U.S. can pursue a hotter, sexier war, senior government officials have told Duffel Blog. The pending divorce is mutual.

The U.S. Military has already released a statement saying, "While we appreciate all the love and support Afghanistan has given us, particularly in justifying our defense budget, after over a decade together conflicts sometimes just get boring and stale. We're not a one-war kind of service."

The U.S. Military has also cited irreconcilable problems with Afghanistan's in-law Pakistan. Afghanistan has listed its own complaints: that the U.S. Military has a wandering eye for "any younger war that doesn't need as much work done. We don't know how the Israelis and Palestinians have managed to keep theirs going for 65 years."

Afghanistan has also complained that the U.S. Military is frequently inattentive to their needs, forgetting their anniversary and giving it inappropriate gifts.

"Last year for our anniversary the Air Force gave us a high-altitude all-weather air superiority fighter," a tearful Afghanistan told reporters. "Our war doesn't even have air combat!" According to Afghanistan, these problems were evident right from the outset of their relationship.

"Our war was always a sham," Afghanistan complained. "Even during our honeymoon, we caught the U.S. Military looking at pictures of Iraq! They swore it had something to do with 9/11, but after just two years they moved in together. After we confronted them, they kept promising to break it off and we naively believed them, but they didn't finally end it until only a year ago."

While Iraq is no longer a factor in their relationship and is in its own controversial relationship with Iran, both the U.S. Military and Afghanistan stressed that their divorce would not impact their other wars, Yemen and Somalia, plus adopted-war Libya. Adoption paperwork on a fourth war, Syria, was halted in mid-2012.

The latest argument was brought on when Afghanistan overheard the U.S. Military bragging about the hot new amphibious assault ship it was producing, and found several provocative pictures of Chinese air defenses in its desk.

When Afghanistan confronted the U.S. Military, the U.S. claimed it was only studying Chinese air defenses because of their connection to terrorism.

Pressed to explain further, the U.S. Military stuttered, "the... uh... Chinese... Islamic... Terrorist... Guys..." and left the room as quickly as possible.

The U.S. Military saw a similar war with Vietnam fall apart in the 1960s over accusations that the U.S. hadn't gotten over its true love, fighting Soviet tank divisions in the Fulda Gap.

USS Haditha Accidentally Sinks Fishing Boat, Machine-Guns Survivors

By G-Had

MANAMA, Bahrain — In a rare setback for the international anti-piracy campaign off Somalia, U.S. Navy officials today admitted that the American warship USS *Haditha* accidentally sank a Chinese fishing vessel just east of Somalia and then inadvertently machine-gunned the survivors.

This contradicted the *Haditha*'s initial report, which said that it had been attacked by seven pirate skiffs and a pair of pirate-operated *Mirage* jets armed with Exocet missiles.

Vice Adm. Mark I. Fox, commander of the United States 5th Fleet, spoke to reporters following reports that a fishing vessel had been "blown out of the water" by "an unusually well-armed warship that happened to be flying an American flag."

Capt. Erik King, the commander of the *Haditha*, claims that his ship was simply following the rules of engagement.

According to the captain, the *Haditha* originally spotted what it thought was a pirate vessel while patrolling 75 nautical miles east of Somalia.

"She was casually steaming up and down the coast with a group of armed men on board, obviously lying in wait for the next innocent ship to steam across her path," King said.

Many fishing trawlers carry armed guards while sailing through Somali waters.

When the *Haditha* demanded the fishing boat stop and be searched, its crew refused, claiming it was a sovereign vessel in international waters.

"Under our current rules of engagement, we're allowed to prevent any suspicious vessels from leaving the area, and that's what we proceeded to do," said King, referring to the *Haditha*'s subsequent attack on the fishing boat with its 5-inch gun, Mark 46 torpedoes, and the captain's 9mm sidearm, which he fired from the bridge.

After the boat sank, the survivors began swimming towards the *Haditha*, prompting King to order all four of the ship's .50 caliber machine guns to open fire on them, as well as launch the ship's SH-60 Seahawk helicopter to drop depth charges.

"They were clearly attempting to board our vessel," said King, "and the rules of engagement allow us to use deadly force to prevent potentially hostile individuals from 'closing with or boarding' our ship, so I'm unclear what the problem is."

According to an anonymous source from the *Haditha*, just before the attack, King also told his sailors that he'd rather "be tried by 12 than be carried by six."

The *Haditha* is an *Arleigh Burke*-class destroyer, designed to operate in an asymmetric environment just off the coast of a hostile or potentially-hostile territory.

The ship has been particularly controversial for its habit of conducting escalations of force on Carnival cruise ships with its Tomahawk Missiles, and of returning captains to their vessels with black eyes and claiming they fell off a ladder.

A YouTube video was also discovered last year showing two members of the ship's crew tossing baby seals off a glacier, although they claimed the seals were already dead at the time.

New Urinalysis Tests Whether Military Members 'Actually Give A Shit'

By El Comandante

WASHINGTON, D.C. — Forget about getting busted for cocaine, weed, or ecstasy — the Department of Defense can now tell if you don't give a fuck.

The Pentagon announced plans Wednesday to roll out a new urinalysis program that will be able to test for apathy. By examining a mere 30 ml of urine, drug testing laboratories can now pick up several forms of "not giving a shit" to include service, command, and subordinate apathy.

Testing positive for service apathy would mean that a service member could care less about being a part of the Army, Navy, Air Force, or Marines. The Coast Guard, however, will be exempt from the new testing because no one really gives a shit if they care or not.

Popping positive for command apathy denotes that a member could "give a rat's ass about anything the commanding officer does or says," while pissing hot for subordinate apathy will expose careerist officers "who step on the necks of their troops for their own personal gain," according to a released memo.

Capt. Nelson Wheez, director of the Navy Drug Screening laboratory in San Diego, California, lauded the new test.

"We finally will be able to detect those individuals who fake it to make it," said Wheez. "The Navy has already incorporated apathy testing into its zero-tolerance policy. Any service member who pops for not caring will be faced with an immediate administrative separation.

"Who knew you could learn so much about someone through their piss," Adm. Jon Greenert, Chief of Naval Operations, told reporters. "This will be a great tool to thin out the force in light of sequestration."

"I show up to work every day on time in a good uniform, shined shoes, and smile while I perform tedious and meaningless duties," said Petty Officer 3rd Class Dee Smith. "I even compliment my division officer for his 'great leadership skills.' Now I have to worry about losing my G.I. Bill if I fail some stupid test that I can't even study for. Shit is weak, player." Even senior enlisted leaders expressed doubts.

"If the old man finds out that I hate his guts and I could care less about the crew at the same time through my urine, it would be awful," said a balding Master Chief who serves on the flight deck of the USS *Carl Vinson*, speaking on condition of anonymity. "Even though I've been retired on active duty for four years, it might be time to really retire."

"All I've ever wanted was to make sergeant 1st class and then I could stop caring," said Staff Sgt. Owen Bright. "This test is really going to screw that up."

Dr. Nehajub Niarjabooba, a leading industrial psychologist, questions the randomness and caring criteria of the apathy test.

"People seem to care more after deployments are over and more on a Friday than on a Monday," said Niarjabooba. "It is highly unfair to state whether a person completely cares or does care a little bit. This test is highly biased to people who care a minute amount as they may not always pass the test's requirement for caring."

At press time, most junior enlisted members of the Army and Marine Corps were seen packing their bags and waiting for their inevitable separation date.

Autocorrect Fail Leads To CIA Waterboarding In Semen

By Addison Blu

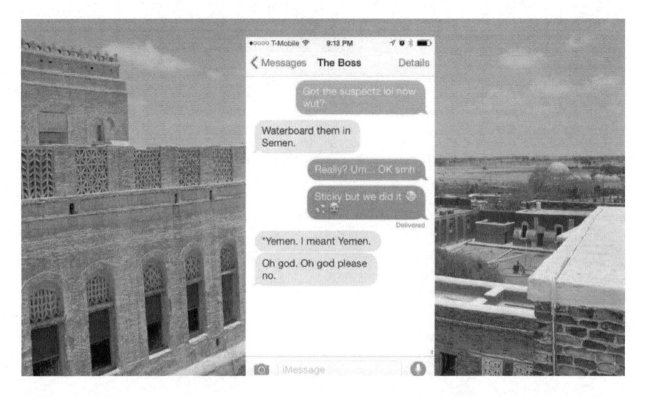

YEMEN — In an Edward Snowden-leaked file recently decrypted by China, secret documents reveal that CIA agents accidentally water boarded a pair of terror suspects in human semen, intelligence sources say. The agents' transcribed depositions were included in the file.

"The text message actually said 'water board the suspects in semen,' not 'Yemen,'" confessed Special Agent "Black." "Give us some credit: we *did* still conduct the semen waterboarding's in Yemen, which is what the boss was trying to say. That's technically a win."

The entire mission was nearly derailed by bad iPhone instructions.

"We almost didn't catch the right guys, either. We were scouring the airport for a duo travelling from London with lesbian ass parts," said Special Agent "Blue."

Black and Blue requested anonymity.

"They already briefed us about the Lebanese passports the day before," said Black. "I guess when we saw the autocorrected instructions we just got caught up in wishful thinking. Stupid Siri."

The agents quickly apprehended their targets after they received improved descriptions of the suspects.

"Texting is the easiest way to update agents," Blue texted Duffel Blog from a disposable cell phone when reached for comment.

"When it comes to transcribing, problems cum with the tertiary. After the interrogation, we had to kill the terrorists, but that part made us feel better. Like the boss is always texting us: Slaughter is the best medicine."

The NSA Is Watching You Masturbate Right Now

By Paul Sharpe

YOUR HOME — You are among the millions currently being watched by intelligence analysts at the National Security Agency as you masturbate alone in your room, sources confirmed today.

Documents leaked by ex-NSA contractor Edward Snowden indicate that at this very moment, your webcam has been activated and has been taken over by NSA Director Gen. Keith Alexander, who is watching and judging you as you click on video clip after video clip of hardcore pornography across numerous websites.

"Oh, this looks interesting," sources confirmed Alexander said from the upper study of his home in Alexandria, Virginia, as he jimmied his pants down to his ankles.

Multiple sources confirming details to Duffel Blog refused to be identified because they were not authorized to speak on-the-record, or they were embarrassed because they climaxed before you.

Like the unblinking red eye of Sauron, Alexander was hungrily fixated on your form and technique mere moments ago as you tired of a clip titled "Sexy Asian with hot ass DP'd" at Redtube and moved on to a POV blowjob clip at Beeg.

Despite initial skepticism, sources confirmed it was indeed you being watched — the person sitting in front of your computer, thinking your tracks were covered since you used an "Incognito" window in Google Chrome.

Matching your rhythm with his right hand, Alexander reportedly used his left to pull up his white undershirt to insert his stubby middle finger into his belly-button, finally climaxing with an audible groan. Sources confirmed Alexander then proceeded to lean in and run his tongue laterally across the surveillance monitor.

Once he climaxed, Alexander's only complaint about his self-pleasuring session concerned the lighting in your room, Duffel Blog has learned.

"Those new 'energy-efficient' bulbs make everything look grainy on my screen. Incandescents were way better," said a sweaty Alexander, as he zipped up his pants. "Thanks, big government."

Duffel Blog reporters Ted Heller and Armydave contributed to this report. The Guardian's Glenn Greenwald also contributed Skype video from Brazil and Spencer Ackerman contributed punk rock lyrics from Washington. The Washington Post's Barton Gellman sulked in the corner while Laura Poitras videotaped the entire scene.

Crusty Old Fuck In The Pentagon Hopes Cold War Just Got Hot

By Juice Box

WASHINGTON – According to sources, that sputtering relic from Basement Level 2B in the Pentagon has been completely beside himself this week, ever since the crisis in Ukraine and the subsequent Russian occupation of Crimea reminded leaders that Russia has a military and that the United States apparently employs people to know about it.

"This might just be the most electric moment in Russian military history since old Gromov resigned in protest of the Chechen invasion of '94," gushed the pathetic bastard, whose name, colleagues say, is Gerry or maybe Tom.

"In fact, I have the point paper to demonstrate the broad geopolitical implications of Putin's brazen grab for power," he added excitedly, to no one in particular.

The man, clearly delusional that developments in Ukraine spell a permanent return to relevance for Russia and the post-Soviet states on the global scene, has reportedly worked as an analyst in the Russia plans and strategy division since 1991. Two-and-a-half decades of utter insignificance later, the daydream believer says he always knew his moment to shine would come.

"Oh my, I have a brief to the general in an hour," the man exclaimed, shuffling through papers and blathering on like he was talking about China or some shit. "This is just how I imagine the eighties, back before we lost our way in that miserable Middle East!"

Convinced the coming months will somehow see a ramping up of militaries or at least escalating tensions resulting in an impossibly elaborate spy game played out on an international scale, the man who boards the Orange Line from West Falls Church every morning says he's ready to give whatever it takes to see this thing through.

"To tell the truth, I predicted exactly this scenario coming to pass at a war-gaming conference back in 2003," he indulged, adding that he might just treat himself to an extra pudding in the cafeteria today.

At press time, the old bag had just gone right ahead and briefed the general, shameless in his Redskins tie and mustard-yellow short sleeves. He might have been stopped, but everyone around honestly thought he was the pay-stubs guy and had no idea where he was going with that folder.

"Was that motherfucker saying something about *submarines*?" the general laughed later.

Lieutenant Promises 'Not To Screw Up' In First Address To Wrong Platoon

By Frederick Taub

FT. HOOD, Texas – A commissioned officer fresh from training and recently arrived at the 1st Cavalry Division made a promise to "not screw up" to soldiers of the wrong platoon, sources confirmed today.

Eyewitnesses barely restraining laughter reported that the visibly flustered 2nd Lt. Matt McGuffin, assigned to 3rd Platoon, stood in front of the 40-strong Headquarters Platoon for several seconds before being able to speak, attempting vainly to wipe his glasses on his ACU blouse.

McGuffin first tried to open his speech with, "Gentlemen it is an honor –er – uh" before noticing a female soldier in the front rank and lapsing into embarrassed stuttering. Finally mustering the personal courage to attempt a salvage of his deteriorating command presence, McGuffin launched a forlorn hope into the breach.

"I am a soldier, I go where I'm told and I win where I fight! Sun Tzu said that," stammered McGuffin, misquoting Gen. George S. Patton to the amusement of his soldiers. "I'm your new platoon leader, Lt. McGuffin, but you can just call me sir! I promise that I'll take really good care of you and I promise not to screw up!"

At this point, Spc. Tom Richards could not resist raising his hand to ask McGuffin where he went to school, leading to a torrent of verbiage from the socially-awkward officer about his time spent at the United States Military Academy at West Point.

"I was a member of the infantry tactics club at West Point, which is kind of like being in Special Forces," explained McGuffin in detail, while the headquarters platoon sergeant made threatening motions at Spc. Richards behind his back. "I remember this one weekend when we went out to the field and the guy assigned to bring the MREs forgot! Boy, we sure were hungry that Saturday. I guess that's what it's going to be like being deployed to the old sandbox, right?"

"You kind of feel bad for the lost little guy," said Pfc. Joshua Ehrenhart of Headquarters Platoon. "I mean, we just got a new PL like, five months ago, so we knew he was talking to the wrong group, but it would have destroyed him if any of us said anything."

"Once he figures out which platoon is his, I'm sure they'll square him away," said Spc. Kyle Peppers as he and another soldier attempted to force a penny into an electrical socket.

2nd Lt. Jesse Davids, the actual Headquarters Platoon Leader, was in fact standing behind the platoon during McGuffin's introduction, though he remained quiet.

"I'll be honest," said Davids. "It surprised me when some other lieutenant came up to my guys and started talking about how he was going to be in charge from now on. I just assumed he knew something I didn't, so I didn't say anything."

At press time, sources report that McGuffin is still obliviously pontificating about "just and unjust wars" and how he will always "lead and calibrate his moral compass in the right direction" even though he got lost numerous times during land navigation training.

US Military Begins Annual Exercise 'Enduring Freedom'

By G-Had

KABUL, AFGHANISTAN – With tensions in the Middle East rising over Iran's nuclear program and the Syrian civil war, the United States and NATO began their largest annual joint-exercise this week, Operation Enduring Freedom.

The exercise is a 365-day event conducted annually since 2001 on Joint Base Afghanistan and involves over 100,000 military personnel from 50 countries as diverse as Albania and Texas, working with another 400,000 host nation forces.

"In an uncertain world, we believe that Enduring Freedom shows that the NATO alliance is still a relevant force," said International Security Assistance Force spokesman Col. Nick Page.

Enduring Freedom features extremely realistic training in small unit warfare, counterinsurgency, aid distribution, government relations, and improvised explosive device handling. The exercise will also eventually feature the successful transition of security operations from ISAF to local forces from the fictional country of GIROA.

While people were amazed at the ultra-realistic training environment, some participants have complained that the exercise was poorly designed.

"Why do we have to keep holding Enduring Freedom in a landlocked country?" complained 5th Fleet commander Vice Adm. John Miller. "I've got a Carrier Strike Group with enough firepower to take on God, but they never get to do anything! And all those [Rules of Engagement], where we can't drop a bomb without seven generals giving us permission. I miss the days when we could just blow the shit out of Vieques."

Some found the exercise vague and confusing.

"This is my third time doing Enduring Freedom," said Sgt. Vince Wegner, "and I'm still unclear what my objective is. Am I supposed to be building mosques and wells, fighting the enemy, removing corrupt officials, or building those same corrupt officials up?"

Col. Page responded: "There is no particular objective associated with Enduring Freedom. We originally tried developing this elaborate backstory involving a massive terrorist attack on the United States, but too many commanders were questioning how that tied in with passing out money to illiterate farmers."

Some independent defense analysts disagreed, saying Enduring Freedom was clearly designed to send a message to China.

"Why else would the U.S. be operating in the middle of Central Asia, hundreds of miles from anywhere important?" asked Oliver Schirmer, an analyst with the Institute for the Study of War.

"No," he continued, "Washington is clearly trying to send a message to Beijing, and that message is: if you so much as twitch at Japan, we will invade your country, topple your government, recreate it using most of the same people, then mull around for a decade while passing out kickbacks until we run out of money and forget why we're even there."

Despite some controversy, many service members are just happy for the training.

"We've done Enduring Freedom so many times it's become a nice refresher for us before we deploy to somewhere important, like Australia or Africa," said Marine Lt. Col. Morris Siegel.

Col. Page added that after 11 years, the United States and its allies were working to keep Enduring Freedom fresh and relevant.

"In a way, we're a victim of our own success because now everyone wants to show off their new hardware in Enduring Freedom. Over the years, we've had to find missions for tank battalions, bomber squadrons, legions of support personnel — things we never would have thought of in 2001 when it was just a dozen guys on horses."

"Last year we got so desperate we started throwing in random scenarios where host nation forces would open fire on friendly forces for no reason," Page said.

Joint Base Afghanistan is a 650,000 km² live-fire range in Central Asia and the largest of its kind in the world. Originally built by the Russians in 1979 over an abandoned British hunting preserve, it was briefly leased by the Pakistani military until it was acquired by the United States and NATO in 2001 for the sole purpose of combat training.

Navy To Apologize To Junior Officer For Shitty First Tour

By Juice Box

WASHINGTON, D.C. – After months of high-profile deliberation, a US Navy spokesperson has confirmed that the military organization is prepared to issue a public apology to Lt. j.g. Jeffrey Hurst for wasting the first two years of his professional life.

"We obviously made a big mistake not recognizing Lt. Hurst's potential sooner," the spokesperson said in a phone interview. "He deserved much better than the assignment he got, and we all feel just awful."

Hurst, 24, who graduated from Auburn University with a degree in English and commissioned through the school's Naval ROTC program, made waves last July when he updated his Facebook status to read, "Accelerate your life my ass… this job SUX!" The post was liked by six of Hurst's friends and received three comments, making it an unmitigated public relations disaster for the Navy.

At the time of the calamitous post, Hurst was serving aboard the frigate USS *Nicholas* as the Electrical Officer, which was reportedly not his first-choice duty, or even his second. The Navy has since relocated him to a holding facility for dissatisfied service members, where he is waited on hand and foot by government servants and allowed to play video games whenever he wants.

"After two years of injustice, I'm glad the Navy is finally taking me seriously," said Hurst, from a massaging recliner in his 600 sq. ft. living quarters. "The scars will remain, but let my experience be a boon to all other service members who aren't getting exactly what they want either."

Hurst, whose education was paid for in full by the Navy, says that despite injuries he will not hold a grudge. "I'd even consider returning to the fleet," he said while being fed grapes, "so long as the Navy guarantees that I won't get yelled at by another XO ever again."

Hurst's previous Executive Officer, Lt. Cmdr. Mark Parsons was relieved of duty and replaced with a teddy bear shortly after Hurst's unhappy story broke.

The Navy's spokesperson said the terms of Hurst's return to service are still under consideration but reiterated the grief felt at all levels of leadership.

According to his Executive Assistant, Chief of Naval Operations Adm. Jonathan Greenert was "horrified" when word got to him that Hurst was displeased with the NICHOLAS.

"As CNO, Admiral Greenert considers it his top priority to ensure that all 400,000 of the Navy's sailors are perfectly content at all times," the assistant said. "Without question, he considers the Lt. Hurst incident a great personal failure."

Greenert himself declined to comment, or at least couldn't because he was too choked up over the whole ordeal. Since the Hurst controversy began, there have been increasing calls in the press for Greenert to step down as the Navy's top officer, and President Obama is rumored to have considered asking the admiral for his resignation.

Hurst's parents, from their home in Columbus, Ohio, say they will reject any apology the Navy offers. "Too little, too late," says Jeb Hurst, 54, who was also a naval officer but remembers having a "pretty good" time. "Our son is a very special boy, and we raised him to know his worth. Thank goodness I'm a Christian man, or I'd give the Navy a good piece of my mind."

Suzanne Hurst, 53, wants nothing more to do with the sea-going service. "Enough pain," she says. "It's time to turn the page on this dark chapter. Time for my Jeffery to finally take a job suitable for a boy of his talents, like astronaut or state senator."

The Navy will issue its apology to Hurst in a press conference next Wednesday.

At press time, hundreds more in the service had stepped forward with allegations of squandered potential and befallen expectations.

CENTCOM Commander, 'Mad Dog' General James Mattis Set To Retire

By Dark Laughter

TAMPA, Fla. – The United States Central Command today announced the resignation of its top commander, Gen. James N. Mattis, who plans to retire from the Marine Corps in a matter of months.

Mattis is best known for commanding the 1st Marine Division during the opening phases of Operation Iraqi Freedom, but has also been criticized by the media for his outspoken opinions and controversial quotes.

Some believe this to be the reason he was passed over for promotion to Commandant of the Marine Corps in 2010.

Mattis, 62, is circumspect about his upcoming retirement. "I postponed my retirement to lead CENTCOM, but it's just time to move on. Years ago, I was called to serve my country by means of conferences and briefings, but I feel like, after forty years of that, I've done my duty."

Mattis, pausing in a dead hang to speak with reporters during a set of weighted pull-ups, continued, "Now it's time to admit that two-hour update meetings are a young man's game, hang it up, and live out my next sixty years as a private citizen back on the world's battlefields, away from the constant stress of the office, like Al Gray would do."

Mattis then effortlessly raised his chin above the bar, in spite of the thirty-five-pound plate hanging from his dip belt.

The decades on the job have taken their toll on the general, a fact immediately apparent as he shuffles into the first of his day's many meetings and briefings.

"What have we got today?" Mattis wearily asks his young aide. "Sir, we have Professor Eugene Shirley Blankenship here from the Geopolitical Military Policy Institute to discuss the historical role of local markets and bazaars as tracers in establishing metrics for the effectiveness of counterinsurgency strategies. He's prepared a hundred slide PowerPoint brief for you."

A nearby rotund man in a tweed jacket then extended a pudgy hand toward Mattis. A look of revulsion immediately spread across the General's face, after which he sprang upon the wide-eyed sociology professor, hurling him against a wall and holding him there with his forearm pressed tightly against the visiting PhD's throat. Mattis was in the process of drawing his pistol when he was restrained by CENTCOM deputy commander Vice Adm. Robert Harward, Command Sgt. Maj. Frank Grippe, and his own aide. After several other staff officers assisted in subduing the aging general, his brow gradually unfurrowed, and he apologized to all present.

"Guess I'm just getting old," Mattis explained.

As he sits in his office hours later, Mattis reflects on how the years have passed by. "When you're young, it's nothing to sit through even a four-hour meeting. You think 'oh, I'm only thirty, I've got plenty of time left to spend killing the enemy,' or 'it's okay, this asshole wasting my time will get shit-canned if I just outlast him, and then I can get back into the field.' But the hours turn into days, the days turn into weeks, then one day you look up and you're 60, still sitting in these goddamn meetings."

Mattis speaks softly as he slowly grinds one of his knives across a whetstone.

"Eventually, you just have to accept that you've reached the limits of what you can do where you are, and it's time to move on to the next obstacle."

The upcoming generation of Marine Corps leadership has expressed eagerness to take up the slack left by Mattis' departure.

"We owe a debt to these old Marines," says Lt. Col. Skip 'Waggles' Wagner, the incoming commander of a Marine fighter attack squadron and recent graduate of the Marine Corps Command and Staff College, "but the fact of the matter is that they're just not suited to the technological nature of product-driven warfare and modern counterinsurgency."

Mattis, who utilizes the radio call sign "Chaos," has repeatedly denied that he has failed to adapt to new technologies, and remains the only living Marine to have killed enemy combatants with non-weapon programs of record, having slit the throat of a former member of the Fedayeen with a large fragment of a broken FEDLOG supply data CD, garroted a Fallujah insurgent with a length of CAT-5 cable being transported to an infantry battalion's communications section, and exsanguinated a foreign fighter from Iran by making a "bone deep" cut down the length of his arm with a laminated cultural smart card bent to form a razor sharp edge.

Mattis admits that the third does not technically indicate a use of technological systems, but notes that he originally attempted to kill the man with a "Phrase-alator" translation device, which shattered after being used to stun the man with a series of softening blows. A planned attempt to crush the skull of a fourth with a "Command Post of the Future" computer was stopped when the general was halted by a civilian field service representative as he attempted to carry it out of a forward Combat Operations Center.

Regarding his plans for retirement, Mattis says he hopes to make more time for his neglected hobbies, which he describes as the study of history and the systematic hunting and killing of enemies "with my own two hands."

"I've got a pretty good area picked out in the [Autonomous Tribal Area] on the border of Pakistan," said Mattis. "I figure it should take a single well-trained squad of fine young men about a month to have the warlords under their thumbs, you know, as long as they don't have a bunch of policies restraining them from befriending the people or killing the enemy. I intend to form and lead that squad."

"Like Al Gray would do," Mattis repeats, staring gravely out his office window at the setting sun.

While somewhat expected, the timing of Mattis' retirement came as a surprise to some, including a few of his colleagues, including Gen. John R. Allen, former CENTCOM deputy and current commander of United States Forces – Afghanistan (USFOR-A).

"Jim's retiring?" asked Allen, seconds before being cornered by several high-ranking members of the International Security Assistance Force to discuss problems with a Memorandum of Understanding for the joint use of a British civilian curry trailer by Marine aviation personnel at Camp Bastion, immediately followed by a three-hour discussion of whether an upcoming joint operation would be best described as mentoring, partnering with, or supporting the Afghan National Security Forces.

"Lucky bastard," Allen added.

BEHIND THE BLOG

Perhaps no other story about Gen. Mattis displayed the larger-than-life character that we built around him than this one. People who know and have served with him know that he's an avid reader, incredibly modest, and rather soft spoken.

We were pretty bummed when he retired in 2013. That was mostly due to the loss to the military, but I'd be lying if I didn't think about the loss of potential Mattis stories. Still, we wrote stories about him in retirement for some time, and he ended up becoming a fan of the site.

In an interview with The Wall Street Journal, Mattis said, "The lads have a well-tuned sense of humor and convincingly imaginative 'reporting' that bode well for a country that could use some laughs. I think the writers know that we need to stop taking ourselves so seriously."

He even gave a rare on-camera interview with CBS News in praise of the site, and later, when he was at Stanford's Hoover Institution, Mattis inserted a line into his bio that mentioned Duffel Blog.

Needless to say, most Duffel Blog writers were pretty thrilled when he was confirmed as Secretary of Defense. Unfortunately, that line in his official DoD bio about being satirized frequently at Duffel Blog is currently missing.

George Zimmerman Tracks Down Joseph Kony, Executes Him

By Skeletor

GULU, UGANDA — Two weeks after George Zimmerman was found not guilty in the murder of Trayvon Martin, the former neighborhood watch captain has turned up in Uganda after allegedly gunning down a "suspicious-looking" African warlord, sources confirmed today.

"Between killing a kid and saving a family, I was getting a lot of press," confessed Zimmerman. "No one gives a shit about Africa except Bono and hipsters. I figured I'd be able to lay low."

While out for a stroll on Sunday evening, Zimmerman spotted Joseph Kony, the rebel leader of the Lord's Resistance Army (LRA) that has terrorized the citizens of Uganda for more than 25 years. The group garnered national attention when a bunch of white college students called for Kony's arrest by volunteering the U.S. military for the job through a sweet film with chill music.

"Look, I don't go looking for trouble," Zimmerman explained. "But there were some people walking around the village who looked suspicious. I was forced to take a stand."

A Special Forces captain whose name is being withheld for security reasons explained things differently.

"I swear every other day I'd have this guy running into my hooch yelling about how somebody looked suspicious. Usually, it was just some villager walking home. Guy is a total asshole."

Despite the captain's remarks, Zimmerman's suspicions led him straight to Kony.

"I knew it was him," Zimmerman told reporters. "He looked really suspicious you know? He was just walking around, wearing a camouflage hoodie, raping women and looking into huts for children he could enslave."

Still, some say Zimmerman was profiling Kony, especially since the behavior he described is common in Africa. "Everyone does that here," explained Moses Hersi, a local villager. "It's practically the national pastime."

"So, I see Zimmerman running at me like a maniac," the Special Forces captain said. "He's yelling about how he's 'got this fucking punk.' We asked him to wait till we could assess the situation but he just took off running."

When Special Forces arrived, Zimmerman was calmly standing over Kony's lifeless body. Asked what had happened, Zimmerman said, "Look every action I took was in direct compliance with Uganda's 'Stand Your Ground' laws. I calmly pulled my sidearm, and after putting Kony on his knees. I shot him in the head. I was well within my rights."

Back at the White House, President Obama reflected on the tragedy.

"You know, had I grown up in Kenya instead of Hawaii, which is totally where I grew up by the way, this could have been me," Obama said. "35 years ago, I could have been kidnapped by Joseph Kony — or I could have been Joseph Kony, kidnapping children."

In Africa, the backlash from the shooting has spread throughout the region. Across the Democratic Republic of the Congo, hundreds of 30-year-old men have been seen wearing shirts reading "We are all Joseph Kony."

Once again, the resulting unrest has forced Zimmerman to move. And a "Justice for Kony" movement has sprung up among confused American college activists who are unsure of how to handle the news of Kony's murder.

At press time, George Zimmerman once again came out of hiding as he saved a family of four when their rickshaw overturned in southern Indonesia. He was unavailable for further comment.

Commander Relieved For Violating Entire UCMJ

By Dark Laughter

CAMP LEJEUNE, N.C. – The Department of Defense has been rocked by the firing and court-martial of a high-ranking Marine officer for allegedly violating every single article of the Uniform Code of Military Justice.

Col. Mitch Grant, once a promising VMI graduate and the commanding officer of the Eighth Marine Regiment, is now charged with adultery, forgery, arson, improper use of a countersign, espionage, stalking, burglary, making a check with insufficient funds, murder, depositing obscene matters in the mail, and conduct unbecoming an officer and gentleman, among other charges.

Grant is only the latest in a string of commanders fired over the past few years for alleged violations of the UCMJ, or civil and criminal laws, including sexual harassment, falsifying records, misusing official funds, bigamy, making sexually explicit videos and showing them to troops, initiating an adulterous relationship and then terminating it by faking their death, negligent handling of nuclear weapons and launch codes, and shoplifting.

These are in addition to numerous other firings motivated by "loss of confidence" that did not necessarily result in charges, but which were sufficiently embarrassing that the Pentagon and armed services wanted to keep their specifics quiet.

Grant laughed throughout the reading of the charges, from chuckling at minor offenses to shaking with uproarious laughter during the reading of more outrageous charges, restrained only by his straitjacket and the wire caged mask over his mouth to prevent him from biting those present in the courtroom.

Officials have declined to disclose the specifics of how the investigation was initiated, but multiple sources have confirmed that it began when Grant was observed with his hands in his pockets before a staff meeting at Camp Leatherneck by Gen. Andrew Blake, who instructed his chief of staff, Col. Patton Callahan, to have Grant report to his office to privately receive a verbal warning.

"Let's just say it was dumb luck that we uncovered any of his crimes at all, and leave it at that," said Callahan. The command initially intended to quietly NJP [non-judicial punishment] Grant so as not to cause any embarrassment, but Grant refused it, insisting on a court-martial instead.

"Refusing NJP was [Grant's] last ditch effort to keep his record clean by staring down the command over the difficulties of convening a court-martial for an O-6," says military legal analyst Joseph Baines.

"I'll be blunt with you. It almost worked. I suspect there were probably many other NJPs Grant avoided in this exact same way. But once the decision was made to go to trial no matter what, and follow the investigation wherever it went, that's when it really exploded."

A Career of Criminal Acts

Though the specifics of the charges have been kept as quiet as possible, so many base residents have been interviewed that some of the incidents have been leaked. Each one seems to involve multiple violations, such as one in which Grant was talking on a cellphone while driving drunk on base, then maimed a pedestrian and fled the scene of the accident. In another, Grant allegedly exposed himself in public while making disloyal statements. After only a few days of charges piling up, the local NCIS office requested augmentation by additional personnel to help catalog them all.

"I think once he knew it was going to trial, at some point it just became a game about trying to violate more of the punitive articles," says Grant's guard, Sgt. Ethan Maynard. "And I think some of us might have unwittingly played along."

"For instance, when the true extent of his crimes was being realized, the bosses elected to transport him back by ship to buy some time to prepare for the trial. That was how he managed to get charged with violating Article 134-10 for escaping custody, not to mention 134-30 for jumping from a military vessel into the water. Oh, and also those two extra murder charges for killing his guards."

"Eventually, seeing all those charges stack up in one case became kind of a running gag," says Daniel Sauls of NCIS. "I don't remember who it was that suggested, as a joke, that we compare his fingerprints with prints on the washers we kept getting reports of in base vending machines. But wow, after that actually panned out, the pieces just started coming together."

"The next day we used voice recognition technology to prove that he was responsible for an epidemic of obscene, racist, and threatening phone calls throughout the area. It was while we were trying to see if he might be involved with the disappearances of some dogs and cats in a neighborhood just off base that we found the cockfighting ring, which was being run by Grant's second wife, a minor he illegally brought into the country as a sex slave and then used to claim fraudulent dependent benefits."

"But the charges that really took us by surprise came when a procedural error during the vending machine investigation caused Grant's fingerprints to be checked against Central Command's biometric database. That's how we discovered 5% of the improvised explosive devices in Afghanistan displayed partial or complete prints. As we reexamined some of the reports related to those IEDs, we noticed they all involved substantial numbers of destroyed weapons. When those weapon serial numbers started showing up in caches of insurgent weapons, the case took on a whole new dimension."

Perhaps the most shocking aspect of the case is not the magnitude of Grant's crimes, but the absence of any documented misbehavior prior to the case. Not only does Grant's service record demonstrate an unbroken chain of outstanding fitness reports, but his trial has already been briefly interrupted by notification of Grant's selection to the rank of brigadier general.

This soon resulted in additional charges of bribery and extortion, as Grant first offered to use general officer rank to benefit his prosecutor if he engineered an acquittal, then attempted to blackmail the court, then the Marine Corps, and finally the Department of Defense, by claiming he would leak the story of his selection to the media if they did not drop all charges. Plans detailing a similar attempt to secure a presidential pardon from Barack Obama were discovered in Grant's cell, along with several vials of heroin Grant was apparently dealing to other prisoners, and a toothbrush sharpened into a stabbing weapon and hidden in a hollowed out copy of Joseph Conrad's *Heart of Darkness*.

"Well, selection isn't exactly the same thing as promotion, strictly speaking," said a visibly shaken Defense Secretary Leon Panetta, during the media firestorm after the story first broke.

Several additional charges of bribery and extortion were originally entered against Grant following revelations of similar appeals and threats Grant made to his former co-conspirators in numerous foreign governments, criminal groups, and terrorist organizations, but his defense attorney successfully argued to have these instances treated solely as charges of espionage and aiding the enemy.

The Problem Of 'Zero Defects'

While the DoD has attempted to paint Grant's apprehension and trial in a positive light, indicating a professionalizing drawdown period after the chaotic expansion necessary for the surges in Iraq and Afghanistan, Baines isn't so positive.

"I think we need to accept the possibility that Grant is only the tip of the iceberg. All the services adopted a zero defects mentality long ago. At first that seems like a great way to ensure the best get promoted. The truth has been very different. But while we've talked for years about the dangers of this producing a culture of mediocre careerists — you know, Capt. Queeg types — we never realized it could also produce something like Mitch Grant. Say what you want about Grant, but he was a decisive risk-taker who mastered the careerists' system, and this made him much more likely to progress up the ranks than a timid mediocrity."

"You know, when you catch a fish this big, part of you has to wonder what else is swimming around down there," he added.

"Death is only the beginning!" roars Grant, frothing at the mouth as he is wheeled out of the courtroom after challenging various officers of the court to duel him, resulting in six more charges of attempts to violate Article 114, which prohibits dueling, and three more violations of articles 88 and 89.

As a commissioned officer, Grant cannot be given a bad conduct or dishonorable discharge if convicted. However, he faces the most serious sentence available to commissioned officers: dismissal. If dismissed, Grant will most likely move on to accept one of dozens of job offers already extended to him by private companies, think tanks, and foreign governments.

In related news, Grant's enlisted driver, Sgt. Adrian Green, has been charged as an accessory following the court's rejection of pleas that he was ignorant of his commander's crimes. Green faces reduction in rank to private, the loss of all benefits to his family, and could be executed as early as next month if Grant is convicted.

Vietnam Veterans Outraged Over Navy Christening Of USS Jane Fonda

By G-Had

WASHINGTON, D.C. – Both the American Legion and the Veterans of Foreign Wars issued a joint statement today condemning the U.S. Navy over the launch of its newest warship, the *USS Jane Fonda*.

"Without getting into Jane Fonda's activities during the Vietnam War, we feel that it is highly inappropriate to name a warship after an actress with no ties to the military," said James Mitchell, a spokesman for both groups.

The ship's name, which had been kept under wraps until right before the launch, was revealed yesterday at a star-studded event presided over by Fonda.

Fonda made a statement prior to the launch, saying, "I dedicate this ship to the brave men who fought and died in Vietnam, especially those in the 66th Viet Cong Regiment."

The actress is extremely unpopular among some military groups for her activities during the Vietnam War, such as posing for propaganda pictures with North Vietnamese soldiers, referring to American prisoners of war as "hypocrites and liars", and more recently cutting the line at a Target in front of a guy wearing an American flag t-shirt.

American warships, traditionally named after states, cities, and posthumous military heroes, have increasingly been named after living figures ever since 1998, when the Republican-controlled Congress named 18 warships in a row after former President Ronald Reagan.

In recent years, the Navy has come under fire for its practice of naming ships after controversial individuals, such as congressional representatives John P. Murtha and Gabrielle Giffords, and civil rights activists Cesar Chavez and Medgar Evers.

When reached for comment, Secretary of the Navy Ray Mabus said that there was no actual law over ship naming conventions.

"Plus, I really liked *Barbarella*," Mabus added.

The *Jane Fonda* will form part of the newly-activated 8th Fleet, built around the aircraft carrier *Hillary Rodham Clinton* (CVN-80), and destroyers *Family Guy*, *Lady Gaga*, and *Trayvon Martin*.

UPDATE - The US Navy has denied any connection between the naming of the *Fonda* and recent negotiations with Vietnam over basing American ships out of Cam Ranh Bay. Navy officials have confirmed however that Cam Ranh Bay will be the *Fonda*'s first port of call and Vietnamese Minister of Defense Phung Quang Thanh was overheard commenting how his country would, "love ship long time."

BEHIND THE BLOG

This was one of those articles that we knew would cause a stir, but couldn't really predict how big it actually would be. As we soon learned, Vietnam veterans really, really, really fucking hate Jane Fonda.

It's no surprise that a large number of those veterans found their way to Duffel Blog and believed every single word of the story. Then they left comments ranging from "kill that bitch" to "kill Mabus" to "kill that bitch and light her on fire."

Have I mentioned Vietnam veterans really hate Jane Fonda?

Entire Military Comes Out Of Closet, Confirms They Are All Gay

By Merrick

WASHINGTON, D.C. — In a shocking turn of events in light of the Supreme Court striking down parts of the Defense of Marriage Act as unconstitutional, the entire United States military has confirmed they are all gay.

"I can't tell you what an unbelievable day this is," said Spc. Jim Ruckers. "Even with Don't Ask, Don't Tell repealed, I wasn't comfortable telling anyone. But after today, I came out, got a boyfriend two hours later and now we're getting married!"

Millions of service-members have flocked to county courthouses across the country to register, in light of the decision to allow gay couples to marry and receive federal benefits. Most however, stood awkwardly in line with their hands in their pockets, avoiding eye contact with each other.

"I'm very happy with my decision," said Staff Sgt. Tim Conway. "My life partner wasn't as thrilled so I told him, 'Look Private, do you want a new Xbox or not?'"

Conway glanced nervously around him. "Uh, that's my way of saying, I love you."

Many throughout the military fear public backlash from opponents to the decision and have refrained from showing public displays of affection.

"Oh no, we'd never do PDA," said Capt. John Stevens. "Actually, we've never even held hands in private because we're saving ourselves for marriage. But we are taking precautions to prevent harassment. Instead of wearing wedding rings, we decided to buy each other brand new Rolex watches."

Critics of the high court's decision believe same-sex marriages will allow abuse of the system, where certain benefits are given to married couples over singles.

"It's offensive anyone would question our motives," said Sgt. Doug Gray, in a heated phone interview. "Our bond was forged in a war. We're more than brothers, we're life partners. Now if you please excuse me, I have to pick my husband up at the BMW dealership."

Duffel Blog spent the afternoon with one happy couple after they purchased their first home together.

"Being single privates in the army, we were forced to live in different barracks," said Pvt. Chris Manning. "But since we're married, we get to live off post together. We shared a foxhole, now we share a home."

"Come on down here," yelled Manning's new husband. "I have something for you, Private Honeybun."

Manning said he'd be right down and jumped off the roof into an Olympic sized swimming pool. At press time, they had met in the shallow end where they toasted their new life with a bottle of Courvoisier.

Outgoing Company Commander: 'I Hate You All'

By Maxx Butthurt

The following is a transcript of outgoing company commander Capt. Vince Williams' change of command speech:

Good morning everyone. I'd normally begin with our unit motto, but after two and a half years of starting every meeting and discussion with it, I just don't think I can stomach it anymore. So, I'll say good morning like a normal human being.

I should probably thank my battalion commander for the opportunity to command this company over the last few years, in both combat and garrison, but I think I'd rather go out into the parking lot and key his car for saddling me with the greatest collection of idiots, malingerers, and criminals that have ever walked the face of this earth.

You'll notice my wife and daughters aren't here sitting in the audience today. That's because Sheila left me six months ago when I had to skip our 10th anniversary trip to Jamaica so I could come in on a Sunday for unit PT, since one of you dipshits decided to go out and get his third DUI.

I wasn't allowed to go to marriage counseling last year when our relationship was on the rocks because the commander had said that soldiers were the priority. So instead I gave my slot to Private Steadman and his former prostitute wife who he met on R&R in Brazil the month prior. Once they got back, she took all his money and Steadman killed himself. So, thanks for that.

Do any of you morons have any clue how much paperwork it causes when you blow your sad little heads off? At least have the courtesy to go AWOL first. But for fuck's sake don't come back for at least 30 days so I can drop you off my books and let someone else deal with the meat sack of failure that is your existence.

This would now be the part of the speech where I talk about our glorious combat achievements. Too bad, there's nothing glorious about walking around Afghanistan for 12 months finding IEDs with your feet. Now I'm deaf in one ear, have almost a pound of shrapnel in my ass, and occasionally I wake up screaming for no fucking reason. But you know what? That doesn't make me a goddamned hero. That was the worst part about coming back. Not my empty home, empty bed, or shattered dreams. No, it was listening to you fuckwads thump your chests and talk about how badass you all were. Did any one of you actually get a confirmed kill over there? One?

I didn't think so.

So, in closing, let me say this. Thank you for the countless weekends I lost with my daughters because I had to deal with your trivial bullshit. Thank you for the two suicide investigations that forced me to cancel training events I'd planned for almost a year. And most importantly, thank you for the dishonesty, poor accountability, and outright theft of almost two million dollars in equipment, which is why I won't be receiving another paycheck until February.

May God smite you all with the power of a thousand suns, and your souls be condemned to Hell for eternity.

And to the incoming commander. Good luck and God bless you for making such terrible life choices.

There's a bottle of scotch in the third drawer of my desk. You're going to need it.

I hate you all.

Outgoing Commander: 'I Still Hate You All'

By Maxx Butthurt

The following address was delivered by Capt. Vince Williams at his Headquarters Company change of command ceremony.

Good morning everyone. I won't start with our battalion motto because the very sound of it makes my stomach curdle and my jaw clench with an unholy rage.

Eighteen months ago, I stood right here and thanked the battalion commander for the privilege and honor of leading an infantry rifle company in combat and in garrison. You all have no idea how happy I was to hand over control of that lunatic asylum. I took some leave and came back prepared to spend my last six months in the Army behind a nice comfortable desk up at the Division Headquarters waiting for my unqualified resignation to process.

After command was over I had managed to convince Sheila to come home with the girls, and we were working on repairing the train wreck that my marriage had become. We'd even started sleeping in the same bed again. I had also started a nice routine with my AA group off-post, and was clean and sober for almost three weeks. That was when I got the call that the HHC commander had been caught making inappropriate comments on his personal Facebook page and that I would be the new commander.

Let's fast forward 10 months to today. I stand before you all a broken man. These soldiers are the refuse of society. The overweight, the battalion staff, the felons, and the drug addicts. No human being should have to endure what I have gone through over these last months. I had been in command seven hours when I got my first phone call... from the ATF! My mortar platoon sergeant had decided to sneak away from a training event and try to sell his 60mm tubes to an undercover agent who he thought was a domestic terrorist.

And don't get me started on the staff. Technically I'm a commander, but what does a commander do when someone outranks him and refuses to come to work, is 19 pounds' overweight, and has a rater who is also his drinking buddy so he'll never get a negative counseling in his life? I'm looking at you, sir.

The real highlight of my tenure as the HHC commander was when I had to come in on Christmas to explain why my senior medic was caught having sex in the sergeant major's office with the assistant S-2 while she was on staff duty.

We won't even talk about the time my wallet was stolen when I was forced to spend Thanksgiving dinner in my Class A's serving food at the mess hall, or the enormous pile of human shit that someone left in the dayroom two hours before this ceremony.

That's because seeing you all standing before me today, in your clean uniforms and black berets, masquerading as human beings and not the vile hell-spawn you really are, brings a darkness over my soul that can only be fixed with lethal amounts of hard alcohol or a manslaughter charge.

So, to my successor remember this: always lock your door, don't ever go into the barracks at night, for any reason, and never provide information about you or your loved ones to anyone in your unit — ever!

Or better yet, go AWOL. Right now. It only gets worse from here.

This is Havoc Six signing off the net. I still hate you all.

Special Forces Soldier Excited To Train Men Who Will Try To Kill Him In Five Years

By Paul Sharpe

UGANDA — Telling reporters that he "absolutely loves this job," a Special Forces sergeant training Ugandan soldiers in tactics and marksmanship went on to say he's really excited to be teaching guys things they will use against him in about five years.

"This is really the reason I joined Special Forces," said Sgt. 1st Class Frank Bilton, who serves with 3rd Special Forces Group. "It wasn't for direct action missions or high-speed stuff. It's all about giving my future enemy an edge he can use against me."

"It really makes it all worthwhile," he added.

Over the past two weeks, Bilton and his Special Forces "A-Team" have been training the foreign soldiers on scouting and patrolling, defensive operations, marksmanship, and the best way to ambush opponents.

"This stuff will be helpful when they try a coup d'état in a couple years, you know? Really put all our hard work into practice," Bilton told Duffel Blog.

"But I'll tell ya. It's going to be exciting when we walk right into an ambush these guys are setting up. Should be pretty interesting."

It's not just boring tactics and military-style training either, Bilton says. The team has spent time engaging in cross-cultural sharing and teaching the Ugandan soldiers English as well, training that will come in handy in a firefight when they shout "asshole G.I." in broken English and write propaganda letters for psychological warfare purposes.

"Seeing the look on these guys' faces when they learn something new, when they realize they can eventually kill all of us with this training," Bilton said. "It really makes me proud to be a green beret."

Guantanamo Prisoners To Receive GI Bill Benefits

By Sgt B

GUANTANAMO BAY, Cuba — In a controversial move praised by the international community as a promotion of human rights, the Department of Defense has begun allowing prisoners at Guantanamo Bay to seek Post 9/11 GI Bill benefits.

While these benefits have traditionally been restricted to veterans of the U.S. Military to use in pursuit of a degree, the Pentagon has seen fit to begin allowing GTMO prisoners to enroll in the program.

DoD Spokesman Wesley Manheim said that it was all a matter of fairness.

"The DoD has been doing everything it can to prevent torture from being used against detainees at GTMO. By allowing the detainees to use the Department of Veterans Affairs, we hope to completely crush their souls with bureaucracy, which to be noted, is completely different from torture. I mean hell, the VA does that to our veterans on a daily basis."

When pressed as to how the detainees would be able to use the money, Manheim stated, "Mostly through online courses. Probably Phoenix College. Don't worry, it's not like they'll be able to get a REAL degree."

Eric K. Shinseki, head of the Department of Veteran Affairs, informed Duffel Blog of the details of how the VA would handle the new claims. "Because most 'guests' at Guantanamo Bay have been there nearly a decade and there is no end in sight for their 'visit', the Department of Veterans Affairs is ready to have their claims processed in 12-15 years as per standard operating procedure."

Shinseki also hinted at plans to award the tan beret of the Army Rangers to all GTMO Detainees. When asked the purpose of this, Shinseki commented that "if they're going to represent the Army in the classroom, I want them to look sharp while doing it."

Representatives of the 75th Ranger Regiment released a response to Shinseki's comments: "Seriously, FUCK that guy."

Most prisoners have praised the DOD for its humanitarian efforts.

"Praise Allah," said prisoner TK421, who plans on possibly pursuing a degree in Homeland Security from American Military University. He wrote a statement in Arabic to indicate his excitement.

"لعمل الأصلي بلدي اليمن إلى العودة وثم إيلينوي ولاية في الكيميائية الهندسة أحضربرنامج سوف
العليا الدراسات. في المستقبل وإنني أتطلع إلى زيارة أمريكا للمرة الأخيرة إن شاء الله".

Although emotions surrounding this news have been mostly positive from the prisoners, the news has its naysayers.

"This is bullshit!" cried prisoner SA15-2-12. "I filled out all of the forms like they said and mailed them to my regional office in Spokane, Washington. I was enrolled in school and they said it was fine if I didn't pay up front. Now I've just been dropped from all my classes because my claim hasn't been processed yet and the school hasn't been paid! I'd rather be force-fed pork and be sprayed with a fire hose than wait for the VA to process my claim!"

The program will also be prorated just like the Post 9/11 GI Bill, but based on a detainees' time behind bars instead of active duty time for service members.

Sgt. Bryant Adams took a break from force feeding SA15-2-12 pork while simultaneously spraying him with a fire hose to speak to Duffel Blog. A National Guard Military Policeman from Mississippi and guard at GTMO, Adams expressed concerns about the fairness of the program.

"It's pretty fucked up if you ask me. This is my third goddamn deployment, one to shitty fucking Iraq and one to even shittier Afghanistan, and now I'm here guarding these stench-covered nerf-herders and I'm only entitled to 80% of tuition and the monthly stipend because I only have two years on active duty orders! IQ19-8 in cell 523 has been rotting in here for nine years so he gets 100%? This is horseshit!"

BEHIND THE BLOG

This was one of those articles which did modestly well. We posted it, it caught the eye of a few thousand readers, and we moved on.

That was in October 2012. Now fast-forward to February 2013, when all of a sudden, there's a ton of new traffic flowing into the Guantanamo story. It was due to an article written by Spencer Ackerman in Wired Magazine's "Danger Room" national security blog. Headline: "Senate Minority Leader Fooled By Report In Military Version Of The Onion."

Oh. My. God.

Ackerman had obtained a copy of a letter sent from McConnell's office to the Pentagon, asking to review the matter of Guantanamo prisoners getting GI Bill benefits, since a constituent had complained. "I would appreciate your review and response," the letter read.

It was signed by McConnell, though it included initials below his signature which indicated it was written by a staffer. We're not sure who "ncm" is — but it's doubtful they still have a job.

Following on the Wired report, the story blew up in national media. It ran the gamut on national news sites with brief mentions here or there, while MSNBC basically dedicated their entire day to it. Lawrence O'Donnell was practically frothing at the mouth during an 8-minute segment on the story.

It was, by far, the biggest "get" for Duffel Blog. But we have our sights now set higher: China or North Korea. We can do it. I just know we can.

First Female Army Ranger Brags About Her Veiny, Seven-Inch Clitoris

By Dick Scuttlebutt

FORT BENNING, Ga. — The first woman in history to graduate from Army Ranger School, arguably the most grueling, toughest training in the U.S. military, and thus the world, has just pinned on her Ranger tab — and she is letting the world know how proud she is of her very large clitoris.

1st Lt. Penny O'Keefe, who was also one of the first females to pass the Army's Infantry basic training course, told a group of reporters assembled to witness her historic graduation all about her genitalia.

"Glass ceilings and good-ole-boys beware," O'Keefe said, smiling broadly. "You might be used to Rangers having big swinging dicks. But this Ranger," she said, pointing to herself, "has a clitoris. A veiny, throbbing, seven-and-one-quarter inch clitoris."

"Plus, it leaks a white fluid when she gets excited," said her boyfriend, Navy SEAL Bleys Pasquale, running a hand through his exquisitely-gelled hair. "It's hot," he added, squeezing O'Keefe playfully.

This kind of talk may seem vulgar to some, but in the Rangers, which is the cream of the crop in the special operations community, it is considered commonplace to engage in rough talk. And O'Keefe can be forgiven for indulging in the practice — that bad-talking lieutenant just became an inspiration for millions of women around the world, putting to rest hundreds of years of sexist exclusion and inequality in the military.

Pasquale, her boyfriend, is more supportive than most men in the military would be.

"It doesn't bother me that she has a hard-charging spec-ops job," he said, gesticulating effeminately and brushing lint off his teal capezios. "I love having a tough little hard-bodied butch girlfriend. It might make some guys feel inadequate, but I'm a SEAL and I wax every inch of my body, so I don't think it'll be a problem for me. We'll probably have some great celebration sex tonight too."

"Only not too much. It makes my butthole hurt after a while," he added.

Fellow Ranger School graduates had high praise for O'Keefe.

"I was really impressed with the way she performed in the SERE portion," said Staff Sgt. Juan Gonzalez, an artilleryman from 3-319th Field Artillery. "She lasted longer than any of us, because when the instructors got close with their tracker dogs, Ranger O'Keefe covered herself in period blood to hide her scent. It threw the hounds off long enough for her to slip away and last out in the woods another 12 hours before they got her."

O'Keefe received a phone call from President Obama the day before her graduation, congratulating her for blazing a trail in military equal opportunity and thanking her for setting such an important example. The White House tweeted its congratulations as well, in addition to its commitment to sending openly-gay and transgendered soldiers to Ranger School in the future.

O'Keefe will report to her first Ranger assignment at Fort Stewart, Georgia, early next month and will likely lead a platoon of Rangers in combat in Afghanistan soon.

Judge To Justin Bieber: Join The Marine Corps Or Go To Jail

By Lee Ho Fuk

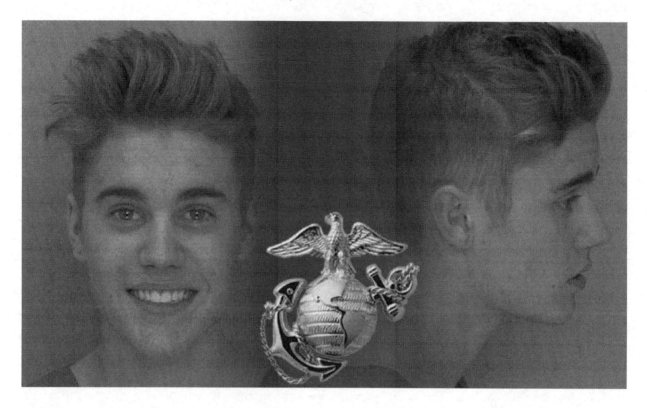

MIAMI — A Miami judge is giving troubled pop star Justin Bieber a choice in punishment following his arrest on Thursday: Join the Marine Corps or go to jail.

Bieber faces charges of drunk driving, resisting arrest, and driving without a license. He also reportedly refused to cooperate with officers on the scene and used "choice words" when police tried to question him and administer a cursory pat down and field sobriety test.

Judge Joseph Farina reviewed the charges and the arrest report which details a litany of belligerence and profanity directed at police. "I ain't got no f------ weapons," the report quotes Bieber as saying. "Why do you have to search me? What the f--- is this about?"

Bieber, a 19-year-old who was tragically discovered after posting a video to YouTube of himself, may soon be joining the ranks of Marine recruits.

"You milquetoast Canadian entertainers think you can come down here and have the run of the place, don't you?" said Judge Farina. "Well, you've finally crossed the line sir. You want to know what this is about? It's about consequences now. You don't have any weapons? Well, you're about to."

The Judge then offered the teenage pop star a choice. He could serve time in a Miami jail followed by deportation to Canada or Guantanamo Bay, or he could report to Marine Corps Recruit Depot, Parris Island for recruit training.

"This is really a terrible choice either way," said Katherine Merriman, an attorney following the case. "This puts Bieber in the position of choosing between terrible treatment in prison from criminals or terrible treatment in the Marine Corps by lance criminals and senior staff."

A stunned Bieber was escorted from the hearing accompanied by Miami police. He has one week to decide what he'd like to do.

Fans gathered outside Bieber's Long Beach mansion expressed guarded support for the singer.

"I know he will be, like, a totally awesome Marine soldier," said Tiffani Liebgott, 15, "and will look totally hot with that green beret!"

"Yeah," agreed her friend, Melani Carson, also 15, "and they also carry those sexy swords like in those commercials. Hashtag 'the hotness,'" she added, actually saying aloud the word "hashtag."

Upon hearing the news, Drill Instructors at Parris Island were reportedly having difficulty properly wearing their uniform trousers over their enormous erections.

Paul and Dick Scuttlebutt also contributed reporting.

Dozens Wet After Coast Guard Cutter Capsizes Off Florida Coast

By Ron

CLEARWATER BEACH, Fla. — Coast Guard Cutter Viking capsized off the Gulf Coast of Florida Friday, leaving all 34 of its crew members soaked and irritated.

At approximately 5:45 p.m., an unidentified piece of mechanical equipment exploded in the boat's engine room. The force of the blast blew a hole into the hull. The boat immediately turned onto its side and would have likely overturned had it not hit the sea floor.

"It was awful," said Randy Myers, who witnessed the explosion while at the beach with his children. "Out of the corner of my eye I saw a big flash, and then a second later heard the boom. The boat went down right away, man. Then I saw the lifeguard tear ass down the beach into the water and run out to the boat."

Myers was at the beach playing volleyball with his daughters, Kendra, 12, and Monique, 14.

"When we realized that people might need help, me and the girls waded out to the wreck. But by the time we got out there, everyone on the boat was already walking back to shore, so me and the girls just kind of encouraged everyone, you know, telling them they didn't have far to walk. Luckily, with this heat wave, the water temperature was pretty comfortable."

Coast Guard spokesperson Jenna Wrigley said that all crew members were dried off immediately and are recovering at home with their families or at Shooter's Bar and Grill for dollar draft night.

Witnesses say the boat captain, Cmdr. Jonathan Crowley, initially attempted to go down with the vessel. After he realized that the boat had sunk as far as it could go and he still remained dry, he jumped into the water and joined his crew in the long walk to shore.

The boat remains on its side off of Clearwater Beach. Coast Guard rescue personnel are waiting for the tide to go out. When it does, a handful of the command's strongest personnel will walk out to the boat and carry it back to shore.

This is the worst Coast Guard tragedy since February of 2007, when 23 personnel at Coast Guard Air Station Houston contracted food poisoning from undercooked hamburgers at a barbecue fundraiser.

BEHIND THE BLOG

Whenever people ask me what my favorite Duffel Blog story is, I usually bring up this one. There's something about this article that I just love. The writer, Ron, was unique among contributors on the site, because he wasn't really an in-your-face joke writer. He had this very dry sense of humor that really shined through on the page.

That line, to this day, still has me rolling: "all crew members were dried off immediately and are recovering at home with their families or at Shooter's Bar and Grill for dollar draft night."

Semper Pink: Gay Marines Protest Possibility Of Female Infantry

By G-Had

SAN FRANCISCO — The premier advocacy organization for gay infantry Marines released a statement today condemning the Marine Corps' plan to open up the Infantry Officers Course to female volunteers.

The San Francisco-based group *Semper Pink* called the plan "an affront to the traditional Spartan values which we cherish as Marines." The group also said that female grunts "will damage the closeness, intimacy, and brotherhood that comes with infantry life."

In mid-April the Marine Corps announced plans to open up an indeterminate number of slots at its Infantry Officers Course in Quantico to female volunteers. In addition, the Marine Corps is developing physical fitness tests to establish gender-neutral standards for grunts. Previously, women were only allowed to serve in non-combat roles.

Semper Pink spokesman Sgt. James Wagner, wearing a shirt that said "I keep my unit out of women, so keep women out of my unit," said that allowing women into the infantry would force gay Marines to deal with lifestyle choices which they disagreed with.

"Plus, we didn't join up to look at some nasty poon-tang!" he emphasized.

Wagner also said that female infantry would be disruptive to unit cohesion.
"Suppose I happen to be out in town, and I see a male and a female Marine from my fire team kissing," he says. "Now any time we're in combat I'll have to wonder if he's thinking of cradling me in his arms as I tell him that I love him with my last dying breath, or her skank ass."

Reactions among other gay active-duty Marines were equally negative.

"There is no way to describe how offended I am," said Staff Sgt. Tim Miller, a drill instructor at Marine Corps Recruit Depot San Diego who previously served as a TOW Gunner with 3rd Battalion, 5th Marines.

"After almost twenty years of protesting and marching, we finally get access to the greatest sausage fest on the planet, and within six months the Marine Corps totally screws it up."

Lance Cpl. Evan Smith, a Rifleman with 3rd Battalion, 1st Marines, believed that female grunts would detract from the Marine infantry experience.

"We had a car wash last week, and I was super pumped to show all the guys the new 'Balls of the Corps' tattoo I got on my chest. But they spent all their time staring at this female Staff Sergeant who's training with us."

"If you ask me, females just can't do the same work as males," he added. "It's basically a question of PT."

1st Lt. Nate Wallis, the first openly-gay platoon commander in the 1st Marine Division, was more circumspect.

"The Marine Corps is all about tradition," said Wallis, "so change doesn't come naturally to a lot of people. However, while the infantry has been gay ever since the Spartans, I think it's time we step out smartly and into the Twenty-First Century."

"Still, someday I'll tell my kids how good we had it in the Old Corps," he mused.

Applebee's Declares Bankruptcy After Offering Free Alcohol For Veterans Day

By Drew Ferrol

KANSAS CITY, Mo. — The president of Applebee's International, Inc. announced Tuesday that the family restaurant chain would be declaring Chapter 11 bankruptcy next week, after offering military service members and veterans free alcohol for Veterans Day.

The promotion resulted in a massive single day loss of nearly $6 billion.

"I just wanted to do something for the troops," said Michael Archer, Applebee's president, in a press conference. "I figured they would come in, be respectful, and have a drink or two. It's not like people go to Applebee's to drink."

Soon after the deal was announced, word of free alcohol spread across social media. Army Brig. Gen. Robert James announced the deal on Twitter, along with the hashtag #CrunkAtApplebees. The tag began trending quickly, after Pentagon spokesman George Little tweeted, "Oh fuck yeah! #CrunkAtApplebees tonight bitches. Join me and Chuckie H!"

"I knew this might be a problem right after the east coast locations opened," Archer said. "I got a call from the Norfolk VA regional manager who said all our restaurants were packed to capacity with lines out the door."

One Applebee's reported the captain of the USS *Theodore Roosevelt* (CVN-71) brought his entire crew to the restaurant, with 3000 sailors fighting for just 100 seats.

"The bartenders and servers fled the premises, leaving the sailors free reign over the bar," said Archer. "The restaurant was on fire five minutes later."

Any location near military bases suffered a similar fate. Security footage of a Jacksonville, North Carolina Applebee's showed hundreds of Marines drinking, head-butting walls, and holding one-armed pushup contests. Marines later spray painted "USMC" and "Wagner loves cock" over the walls.

"Three guys came in and sat down at the bar," said Michelle Baxter, a bartender at an Applebee's in Butte, Montana. "They ordered three kegs and finished them in half an hour. One of them died for a moment. Actually died. He fell to the floor and wasn't breathing. The two others did CPR on him while shouting 'Wake up pussy, there's beer left!'"

"He got back up and started drinking again. He wouldn't go to the hospital unless he could bring his keg," she added.

Although going out of business, Archer says he has no regrets. "I wanted to thank our veterans. They really are our nation's finest men and women. They proved it yesterday."

GNC To Release Pre-Workout Dip

By Erik Sullivan

SAN DIEGO, Calif. – Sports nutrition giant GNC plans to release a new pre-workout smokeless tobacco product some time in 2015, Duffel Blog has learned.

The experimental energy/nicotine product, codenamed "Tobaccosplode," was designed for the warrior/athlete market niche that pervades the armed forces.

"Dipping and abuse of pre-workout supplements are both cultural trademarks of the military," a GNC internal memorandum says. "By combining the two, our company hopes to help America field a force of stronger, angrier warriors with a litany of bizarre heart conditions."

Human trials of the new product conducted at Marine Base Camp Pendleton have yielded overwhelmingly positive results. Marines and sailors who used the Tobaccosplode reported that it significantly increased their desire to "get their fucking pump on."

Paradoxically, users also reported profound erectile dysfunction, paired with a nearly pathological explosion in libido, resulting in a 600 percent increase in incidents of Marines dry humping inanimate objects and/or their battle buddies.

"Greatest product ever!" an anonymous test subject raved on an evaluation form. "I've added 100 pounds to my leg press in under a week, gave myself tennis elbow from high-fiving my bros so much, and instead of sleeping, I just throw in another dip and start roundhouse kicking shit in my house."

Tobaccospode works through a proprietary blend of supplements and a hybridized strain of nicotine derived from the botanical fusion of tobacco and poppy flowers grown in a medium of gunpowder, bull fertilizer, and bald eagle claws.

Along with the nicotine blend, codenamed "Max Nicoffeinol," the dip also includes Creatine, Taurine, Semenine, L-Citrulline, L-Arginine, L-Powernine, Rad Dopeanine and Splenda. Chemical absorption of Max Nicoffeinol through oral cell membranes is expedited by GNC's proprietary blend of added fiberglass and porcelain shards, which cut a bunch of holes in your mouth so the dip can just shit drugs right into your bloodstream.

One "three-fingered pinch" of Tobaccosplode is the recommended dosage for any one hour period of normal activity, or "one every 2-3 sets" when conducting strenuous exercise. Use during exercise is guaranteed to eliminate fatigue, increase gains, maximize swol, and improve yell volume during heavy reps.

GNC's projected price point is $11.99 per can with a recommended 240 can maximum intake per 30-day cycle. Cycling off Tobaccosplode, however, is not recommended. Always use a spitter when using Tobaccosplode, as the expectorate byproduct is extremely toxic. Side-effects of use may include insomnia, weight loss, Swedish accent, manic malaise, explosive pregnancy, urinary diarrhea, detachable skin, fur tongue, cancer and frostbite.

Tobaccosplode will come in four different flavors; Wintergreen, Sexual Tyrannosaurus, Fudge Brownie and America.

Total Asshole At Operations Meeting Asks A Question

By Paul Sharpe

THE COMPANY OFFICE — A complete and total fucking asshole that everyone wishes would just die already actually has a goddamned question at the end of the operations meeting we've been in for six fucking hours, sources confirmed today.

Responding to the battalion commander's request for anyone to speak up "if they have any saved rounds," sources confirm that piece of shit 1st Lt. Nathan Benjamin actually opened up his goddamn cum dumpster instead of keeping it shut so we could get out of this godforsaken room.

"Yeah sir, I just have a quick question," Benjamin reportedly said, indicating he had a simple question but you know goddamn well it's going to turn into some super-long bullshit that's going to delay us another hour. "What's your guidance on what to do if the main effort of the patrol comes under fire?"

Sources confirmed that some in the room looked over at him and unfortunately were unsuccessful at trying to murder the lieutenant with their eyes, while others muttered, "Oh my fucking god, the QRF comes to the rescue, asshole!" under their breath.

"Well, lieutenant, that's a good question," said the battalion commander of what everyone in the room knows damn well was a totally shitty question. "As I said earlier, the QRF will be called up if things get a little too hairy."

"Let's pull up the route and possible points of enemy contact again just so we're all on the same page," said the battalion commander, before saying the same goddamn bullshit he said about two fucking hours ago.

At press time, multiple people in the room were seen in their daydreams pulling out nickel-plated .45 caliber pistols and shooting the lieutenant right in the fucking face because he needs to die right fucking now.

Department Of Defense To Award Purple Heart For Butthurt

By Epic Blunder

WASHINGTON – In the wake of the newly unveiled Distinguished Warfare Medal, the Department of Defense intends to relax standards on the nation's oldest military decoration – the Purple Heart. Under the expanded interpretation, the award will now be available to any disgruntled service member suffering from disillusionment and shattered expectations.

"Acute Rectal Inflammation, colloquially known as 'butthurt,' is a serious and grossly underrated epidemic plaguing our military," Lt. Jimmy Chang, Doctor of Osteopathic Medicine, told Duffel Blog.

"Essentially, psychological or emotional trauma, stemming from either internal or external stimuli, manifests itself and eventually begets anal trauma. In severe cases, butt cells can become so hurt that they become malignant. In fact, butthurt is the leading cause of colon cancer among service members."

Established by George Washington in the aftermath of the Revolutionary War, the Purple Heart is awarded to service members wounded or killed by enemy action. The Pentagon exercised "great prudence and foresight" in redefining "enemy action" to accommodate the majority of service members who never have and never will see combat.

"Startling new data reveals that up to 98 percent of service members are dissatisfied with their lives and hold resentment of some sort towards the system and their superiors," continues Chang. "Conversely, the remaining two percent experience unparalleled levels of enthusiasm and job satisfaction. We call them 'lifers.' They suffer from an irreversible condition of their own."

According to osteopathic theory, the "feel good" sense of self-importance, accomplishment and long-overdue justice evoked from the receipt of the Purple Heart will cause negativity and ill-will to subside by engendering warm and fuzzy feelings of appreciation and self-esteem.

Butthurt service members can apply for their Purple Heart online by clicking on advertising banners posted on Facebook and can expect it to arrive within six to eight weeks after filling out a brief grievance questionnaire for any slight, real or perceived, and paying for shipping and handling.

"It's really our way of patting our guys on the back and saying, 'We're not going to change anything, no matter how much you bitch, but thanks anyway,'" a Pentagon spokesperson said in a statement. "If you don't feel better after you get your Purple Heart, then maybe the military just isn't for you."

The first 1,000 applicants will also receive a free suppository.

Decorated War Hero, Airborne Ranger Emasculated By Wife At Local Mall

By Armydave

KILLEEN, Texas – Sources confirmed that earlier this afternoon while sitting outside of a dressing room in a mall boutique, decorated soldier Samuel Williams was publicly dressed down by his 24-year-old wife.

Williams, a staff sergeant who once killed a man with his bare hands, is an Airborne Ranger that has spent five of the past seven years in Iraq or Afghanistan. His wife, Jennifer Williams, works at the post commissary and is planning to go back to school to be a radiation therapy tech "or something like that."

According to reports, after taking his wife out to "a nice lunch to spend some time together before his next deployment," the couple went to the mall to pick up a few things for the baby they recently learned was on the way.

Shortly after arrival, Mrs. Williams spotted a cute little black dress in a window storefront and tugged at her husband's arm with a wide grin in an effort to pull him into the store. After hesitating, Williams relented and followed his wife inside, where he then passed the time on a little bench by reading the latest edition of Cosmopolitan and silently recounting the many horrors which he had personally lived through.

"Hey, babe? Can you go out there and get me this in a size three?" Jenny Williams said as she tossed a dress over the dressing room door. "Hey?! You there? Jesus, Sammy. Go get me a size three already!" she added from within the dressing area with a stomped foot.

Williams, the top graduate of his class in Ranger school, dutifully stood up and meandered over to the dressing room. He took the discarded dress. Head down and lip out, he shuffled aimlessly throughout the store in search of a cute little striped number in a size three – all the while carrying his wife's purse. Before reaching the dress rack, a dull thud could be heard as his testicles fell out of the purse he was carrying. With a defeated sigh, he leaned over, picked them up, blew off the dust, and stuffed them back into the handbag.

Williams confusedly stared at the dress rack for a long moment in an effort to avoid the judgmental eyes of the shop's other patrons. Ultimately, he returned with a size five, knocked on the dressing room door, and placed the dress in the dainty hand which appeared.

After a moment of silence, a howl emanated from the dressing room occupied by Mrs. Williams. The door swung open, and the petite woman stomped over to her husband — a man who once dropped three Iraqi insurgents at approximately 1,100 yards — sat dumbly and stared at her.

"I asked you for a size three! You think I'm so fat I need a five?" she demanded with her hands on her hips. "Either you think I'm fat or you're just stupid!" she added.

Silver Star recipient and "hardcore, airborne motherfucker," Williams opened his mouth to say something, but only one sound emerged.

"Urmmmm," he said.

This response infuriated Mrs. Williams. Her eyes went wide, and she threw the dress at the Ranger before screaming into his face.

"You aren't even paying attention to me! This is supposed to be our special day! I'm not fat! You don't know what I have to do all day, sitting at home cooking all the meals and taking care of our children. I swear, all you are good for is waking me up at three in the damn morning by screaming and hollering in your sleep! You're useless."

Mrs. Williams then stormed out of the dressing area, through the boutique, and into the mall. Williams sighed gently to himself and stared at the floor. After a moment, he pushed himself up, which was made difficult by the ragged shrapnel embedded in his right kneecap. He quickly jogged after his wife.

During a hushed conversation in the mall's food court, Williams apologized to his wife as she ate a slice of pizza from a paper plate.

"This pizza is so disgusting," complained his wife. Upon hearing this, Williams' mind wandered to the time he had to eat his dead battle buddy after being stranded behind enemy lines in Kosovo back in '99.

After their snack, Williams hugged his wife, promised to pay more attention to her, and the couple returned to the boutique where they purchased the size three.

Military Pushes For Same Broad Rules Of Engagement As Civilian Police Forces

By Erik Sullivan

KABUL, Afghanistan — Senior American commanders in Afghanistan are pushing for more permissive Rules of Engagement to put their troops on par with domestic law enforcement, Duffel Blog has learned.

"Just because we've changed the operation name doesn't mean this isn't still a war," Gen. John F. Campbell, commander of American forces in Afghanistan, said at a joint press conference. "If we're going to permanently pacify an entire population, we need to think less like the UN, and more like the NYPD."

Large civilian police departments like those of New York City, Chicago and Los Angeles, have long been the envy of more aggressive military units.

"I've always dreamed of joining Albuquerque SWAT," Staff Sgt. Brian Anderson, currently on his 5th deployment to Afghanistan with the 75th Ranger Regiment, told Duffel Blog. "I just really want to fucking shoot someone."

The consensus among troops that they have been hamstrung by mincing, limp-wristed bureaucrats is as ubiquitous now as it was in the latter years of the Vietnam War. According to a Pew Survey of deployed personnel, a staggering 91 percent replied 'agree' or 'strongly agree' when asked for their response to the statement, "My job would be easier if I were allowed to choke people to death for no reason."

"Right now, I've got a bunch of Cosmo-sipping congressmen and self-serving, careerist POGs telling me how to do my job," said Capt. Miles Corgan of the 10th Mountain Division. "If my guys could be even half as aggressive as a small-town cop, this war would have been won in '07."

According to an internal memorandum obtained by Duffel Blog, the initial phase of the plan is already underway. CIA operatives are engaging with members of the Afghan Loya Jirga to distribute large quantities of crack cocaine to the country's poor population while simultaneously introducing stricter drug laws. The tactic is "time-tested and stunningly effective in other countries," the memo states.

Furthermore, a small pilot program of Police Advisory Teams, comprised entirely of police officers in National Guard infantry units, have been operating in the capital since the summer of 2014.

"Best kill teams I've ever worked with," said Ibrahim Maqal, an Afghan National Army Commando. "Those dudes will earhole a kid for picking up a rock. My dream is that law enforcement in Afghanistan can someday be as free and liberal as it is in America."

Meteorologists Forecast Bowe Bergdahl Shit Storm

By Lee Ho Fuk

WEATHER WARNING #06-02
REQUEST WIDEST DISSEMINATION TO ALL UNITS IVO THE INTERNETS

SHIT STORM WARNING

VALID TIME: 140602/1330D (140602/0900Z) - 140602/1930D (140602/1500Z)

FORECASTER: CWO WEINER/METOC/TACC/DSN: 357-6666

HIGH SPEED SHIT STORMS ARE OCCURRING OR ARE FORECASTED TO OCCUR WITHIN 10NM OF
TWITTER, FACEBOOK, AND ALL ASSOCIATED SOCIAL MEDIA. FORECASTED WINDS ARE FROM
230°V290° AT 12-18 WITH GUSTS TO 23-27KT ISOLD 30KT. THE POTENTIAL FOR VISIBILITY
REDUCED TO LESS THAN 5SM BUT GREATER THAN 3SM EXISTS DURING PERIODS OF BLOWING
SHIT. TAKE PRECAUTIONS THAT WILL PERMIT ESTABLISHMENT OF AN APPROPRIATE STATE OF
READINESS.

SALSA NIGHT AND THE DAVE ATELL / CLEVELAND BROWNS CHEERLEADERS (THE BROWNEYES)
USO SHOW ARE MOVED TO HANGARS 4 AND 6 DUE TO INCLEMENT WEATHER.

A LOW-PRESSURE SYSTEM OF JOURNALISTS REPORTING BOWE BERGDAHL AS AN AMERICAN HERO IS EXPECTED TO CRASH INTO A POWERFUL STORM OF SOLDIERS WHO SERVED WITH HIM AND CALL HIM A DESERTER AND TALIBAN COLLABORATOR.

FECAL MATTER IS EXPECTED TO ECLIPSE ALL OTHER NATIONAL SECURITY ISSUES, THE VETERANS ADMINISTRATION DEBACLE, THE ONGOING WAR ON TERROR, F-35 ACQUISITION, OUTED CIA CHIEFS, IRS SCANDALS, ABANDONED DIPLOMATIC MISSIONS, PENDING ECONOMIC COLLAPSE, AND ANY MENTION OF FALLEN SOLDIERS OR DEAD VETERANS.

TAKE COVER. THIS IS A WARNING. TAKE COVER NOW.

Dempsey Unable To Retire Until CIF Signs Off On Missing Canteen

By Addison Blu

WASHINGTON — Despite Gen. Martin Dempsey having a retirement ceremony last week, the Army Central Issue Facility (CIF) has refused to clear him due to unreturned issue items and has delayed his retirement indefinitely, Duffel Blog has learned.

"The big gen'ral (sic) hasn't turned in his aluminum canteen from 1979 or his medical kit from 1985," CIF clerk Joe Buckley told reporters, noting that having a four-star rank is no exception. "After inflation, the total charges due are about $1,040,000, but the big gen'ral refuses to pay."

Senior defense officials said Dempsey has so far taken the news in stride, confiding to reporters that the general has been seen outside of his garage spraying down a rucksack and a number of items with a garden hose.

"They also kicked back half of my unused equipment for being too dirty," Dempsey said. "And I'll never find the canteen. After checking General Jackson's and all the surplus stores, they didn't have anything from the 1900's."

Still, Buckley and other clerks at CIF are indifferent to the general's plight. The Central Issue Facility, better known as CIF — or as soldiers call it, Satan's Asshole — has rigorous standards for returned equipment, and can levy pay in cases where gear is brought back that is not up to par.

"We can write him a statement of charges, but they'll dock it from his retirement pay," Buckley told reporters, while loading another box of returned CIF gear into an incinerator. "I told big gen'ral to ask his friends if they had an extra '79 canteen, but these disrespectful soldiers don't care enough to take advice."

Since Dempsey has already stepped down as Chairman of the Joint Chiefs of Staff but refuses to accept the charges, he has been reassigned as a staff planner for 1st Infantry Division until his retirement paperwork is stamped by CIF.

Soldier Dies From Massive Erection After Firing .50-Cal For The First Time

By Sgt B

FORT LEONARD WOOD — An Army soldier attending basic training died from a massive rush of blood to his penis after firing the M2 .50-caliber machine gun for the first time, sources confirmed.

Pvt. Alvero Rojas was six weeks into his basic training when his unit went to the range for familiarization fire with several of the Army's crew served weapons.

"Rojas enlisted to become an Admin Specialist but we take all of our basic trainees to the range to fire these weapons to give them an idea of what it's like," said Sgt. 1st Class Alexander Pitts, Rojas's lead Drill Sergeant. "Just because a soldier is slated to end up behind a desk doesn't mean they won't find themselves shooting a .50 or MK19 at some point."

Rojas's death was regretted by his entire basic training company.

"He was liked by everybody in the unit. He always found a way to liven everyone's spirits when training got tough. I know he was so excited to fire the .50-cal," said Pvt. Stephanie Taylor. "All he talked about for the week leading up to it were the weapon system's capabilites. He actually walked around quoting the Army field manual about it."

Witnesses stated that as Rojas began to fire the machine gun, he sprouted an erection which became so large it busted through the notoriously weak crotch seam of his ACU pants. Army medical officials listed his cause of death as priapism, described as "a persistent, usually painful, erection that lasts for more than four hours and occurs without sexual stimulation."

"We probably shouldn't have waited four hours to get him medical attention," Taylor said. "We've all seen the ads, and should've known the risks."

Rojas fired his full combat load before passing out due to the lack of blood and oxygen in his brain.

At first, the company just laughed off the situation, and drew giant erections on his face in sharpie. But when he wouldn't wake up, he was then medevaced to the post hospital where doctors tried furiously to revive him. After several hours of ice baths, being shown pictures of his grandmother in a bathing suit, and having two business men talk to him about Six Sigma, Rojas succumbed to his condition and passed away.

"We tried everything in our knowledge," said Dr. Steven McCanon. "No matter what we did, we just couldn't seem to reverse the effect that firing that weapon had on him."

"I'm always happy to have soldiers excited about training, and getting to shoot the big guns usually gets them pumped up but I never expected anything like this. I'm not really sure what we can do to prevent this in the future or if we even really learned anything here," said Pitts.

Company members have renamed Rojas' weapon ".50-Cialis" in his memory.

Chaos: General James Mattis Announced As Next Commandant Of Marine Corps

By Paul Sharpe

WASHINGTON, D.C. — In a controversial move sure to send shockwaves throughout the Corps, President Obama announced today that Commandant of the Marine Corps Gen. Jim Amos will soon be replaced by Gen. James Mattis.

Amos indicated his plans to resign early — having served only two years out of the four-year term as Commandant — saying that "he's getting too old for this shit."

"I'm just sick of dealing with these savages in the press and in Congress. They keep asking me questions about snipers pissing on people, nazi flags, and other crap," said Amos. "I figure Jim [Mattis] will certainly know how to handle them."

Not one to mince words, Mattis is known for controversial quotes — once telling a reporter that it was "fun to shoot some people," and that his Marines should always "have a plan to kill everyone they meet."

Mattis, who announced his plans for retirement months ago, is being recalled for the position as top commander at a time when the Marine Corps transitions from combat to peace.

"This transition stuff is all a bunch of crap," said Mattis, after returning from a 30-mile ruck run with an 80-pound pack. "Our Corps will always be killing people. Even in peace time, I'll find someone for our boys to kill out there. Yeah, I'm talking to you Iran."

When reached for further comment on his promotion, Mattis was glad that he would be staying in uniform.

"When I announced my retirement, it was at a time when death by PowerPoint was my entire day. I thought I had missed my chance for Commandant," said Mattis, after spitting out his Red Man chew and downing a double-shot of Jack Daniels. "But now that I am receiving this promotion, it means most of my job is to visit our boys overseas — Afghanistan, Djibouti, Libya — and I can get closer to the action again."

Mattis is excited that he can leave the briefing room to get back to "systematically tracking and killing the nation's enemies with his bare hands," but he also has other plans for sweeping changes across the Marine Corps.

"This policy that doesn't allow sleeve tattoos is a bunch of horseshit," said Mattis, as he showed off his own full-sleeve tattoos running down both arms. "So that's the first thing to go."
Another policy change includes tweaks to physical training. While most infantry Marines can probably keep up with the general on runs, Mattis says that he wants everyone to live up to the ethos of "Every Marine a Rifleman."

"These air wingers and admin folks think they are sitting pretty, only heading to the gym or not doing PT at all," said Mattis, in between his third round of 350lb back squats. "So, I'll also be leading them in 15-mile runs until they shape up."

Finally, Mattis says he'll reverse the no-hazing policy that Marines have been under since the nineties, saying that it's "good goddamn training."

"Listen, I don't like stupid shit," said Mattis. "but if you're one of my fine young men about to go on deployment and you have a boot who isn't listening, I think it's a valuable training tool to duct tape him to a bench, mentor on an emotional level with a wall-to-wall counseling session, or make him dig a hole to China."

"I mean hell, that's where we're going [China] eventually anyway. Might as well train like we fight," he added.

Mattis is expected to take command at the beginning of the new fiscal year.

BEHIND THE BLOG

Yeah, I know we retired him in a previous story. But let's suspend reality for a moment. At the time this article was published, the Marine Corps was dealing with Gen. Jim Amos — a fairly unpopular commandant — so we decided to use our powers and make Mattis the top guy. At least he could be commandant, somewhere.

The Photoshop job by Stormtrooper was phenomenal, and there are still, to this day, Marines who think that Mattis has full sleeves running down his arms.

An interesting thing happened after this article was published. I got an email from a man named Tom Mattis, who put in parentheses "yes, that Mattis. Jim is my brother."

The former Marine sergeant and Vietnam veteran said he was a new fan of the site after he read the Mattis as commandant article. So I chatted him up and said I was honored to have him as a fan. He wrote back, "He has a great sense of humor and I am sure he will enjoy it, as does our 90-year-old mother. In fact, it was she who tipped me to your site!"

In a follow-up email, Tom explained that it was their mother who had to explain to a top Air Force general (I won't mention who) what Duffel Blog was. The general, who likely served with Gen. Mattis in the past, called Mattis' mother to congratulate her on her son's big promotion.

"My mom had to tell her it was satire," Tom said.

West Point Professor Always Knew Cadet Would Become A Terrible Officer

By Maxx Butthurt

KANDAHAR, AFGHANISTAN – After savage fighting — much of it hand-to-hand — a brutal Taliban attack on Combat Outpost Hellfire was stopped recently by the heroic actions of the infantry commander on the ground.

While many in the Army are hailing Capt. James Wild as a hero of the battle, his West Point professor maintains that the incident is just another in what he calls "a series of extensive leadership failures."

"I just knew something like this would happen if he was in a leadership position. He didn't have any discipline at all. He was without a doubt one of the worst students I've ever had," said Maj. Martin Sutherland, when asked about the incident.

Now serving as a professor of history at the U.S. Military Academy in West Point, NY, Sutherland speaks from his experiences as an Air Defense officer from 1984 to 1995. His belief is that discipline and standards are of the highest importance to a good Army officer.

"Wild had the worst looking boots in the company. When other cadets were spending their Friday nights shining shoes, and getting their rooms ready for the Saturday morning inspections that I insisted on, Wild would just go out and party. Can you believe that? A 19-year-old kid in college trying to become an officer, and he couldn't even find the time to starch his BDU blouse!"

The distraught man rubs a gnarled hand through his thinning comb-over and shakes his head sadly.

"I feel partially responsible for the whole thing. One day, right before graduation I was conducting one of my standard 5am snap inspections. When Cadet Wild showed up to formation I saw that his BDU belt wasn't regulation issue. Then, when I had the cadets pull up their pant legs I saw that he was wearing white socks. WHITE SOCKS!"

The major is clearly still troubled by the event, years later.

"I pulled Cadet Wild to the side and explained to him why wearing white socks could get his men killed."

The man sighs, and opens a folder he has sitting on his desk.

"Look at all these infractions. Failure to wear his TA-50 according to the SOP, missing drill and ceremony training for tutoring sessions with his military tactics instructor, failure to display proper military insignia in a PowerPoint brief!"

Sutherland was also asked about Wild's physical and leadership abilities.

"Oh, he was always working out. He was on the triathlon and boxing teams. Maybe if he had spent less time training and focused on the important things, like military protocol, marching, or uniform standards then maybe he would have become the officer I'd hoped for. Instead you get something like this," Sutherland says, as he gestures with disgust at the printed-out summary of the battle.

When his isolated outpost was attacked in the pre-dawn hours, then-Lieutenant Wild and his platoon repelled the first wave, killing over 30 enemy fighters in the first few minutes of battle. Unfortunately, dust in the atmosphere, the position of the moon, and civilians within a 4,000-meter radius of the base prevented Close Air Support from being used to support the troops.

Artillery was also denied for the same reasons. The next wave was able to overrun the outer perimeter, forcing Wild and the remnants of his shattered unit to engage the enemy in savage hand-to-hand combat. Reports from the ground confirm that he personally dispatched three enemy soldiers with his entrenching tool, before pushing his men to retake the breached walls of the compound.

During the fighting Lieutenant Wild desperately pleaded for an exception to be granted to the fires restrictions, but the President was out golfing that morning and the required signature of a four-star general officer was unable to be obtained until after the fight had ceased.

When the battle was over, the enemy had been beaten back, but many in Lieutenant Wild's platoon had been mauled.

This week, now-Capt. James Wild and four of his soldiers received the Silver Star for their actions during the fight. Pictures taken after the battle and at the awards ceremony showed Wild wearing white socks.

Maj. Sutherland did not offer any further comment on his most recent infraction.

Military Drawing Up Plans For Nationwide Gun Confiscations

By G-Had

WASHINGTON – A senior U.S. general has confirmed that the military has secretly drawn up plans to round up large numbers of privately-owned firearms from American gun owners.

Gen. James M. Scott of the U.S. Air Force confirmed that the Pentagon received a series of formal directives from the White House between November 7 and December 13 to begin plans for a massive nationwide operation to confiscate guns using a series of federal databases compiled over the last few decades.

Scott spoke with *Duffel Blog* reporters in a parking garage in northern Virginia.

Scott also confirmed that a certain four-star general who heads the U.S. Transportation Command was intimately involved in the planning. General Scott would not reveal the general's name out of concerns for his safety.

The plan, known in the military as Operation PREAKNESS, combines a series of tactics developed for house sweeps and room clearing in Iraq and Afghanistan, which Scott admitted had been used as test-runs for the U.S.

"If we can confiscate millions of firearms in a country where we don't speak the language or understand the culture, the U.S. should be easy," Scott told Duffel Blog. "I just feel sorry for that poor Osama fellow we had to kill to justify the whole thing."

According to Scott, the actual planning for Operation PREAKNESS was initiated in early 2009 and developed in conjunction with the United Nations, Senator Dianne Feinstein, and several other liberal organizations such as the National Organization for Women, Planned Parenthood, Greenpeace, the American Federation of Labor, and the National Rifle Association, which is apparently a front for all the previous groups.

While there was initially some concern about the constitutionality of using the military on American soil, page 2131 of the Affordable Care Act actually amends the Posse Comitatus law to allow the military to disarm private citizens at the direction of the Secretary of Homeland Security. Objections by then-CIA Director David Petraeus were quietly silenced in November.

A test-run for PREAKNESS was actually conducted in early December in Clinger, Pennsylvania. A joint platoon of Army Rangers and UN Peacekeepers, working with select state and local officials and using imagery collected by the Google Street View Car, quietly went door-to-door and managed to collect all the firearms from Clinger owners.

The few owners who did complain were initially transported to Fort Leavenworth in Kansas to explain their case before a special international tribunal, before being sent to the National Center for Gun Control in Guantanamo Bay, Cuba.

A follow-on operation using just the UN Peacekeepers is planned later this week for any owners missed in the previous sweep, although the Peacekeepers have confirmed they will be using a post office truck to infiltrate the area.

Senator Clarifies Remark Telling Troops To 'Go Fuck Themselves,' Says Quote Taken Out Of Context

By Paul Sharpe

PHOENIX, Ariz. — A state senator is in hot water after making controversial remarks last week in an interview with *Arizona Foothills Magazine*. The full interview, which is to be released Friday, includes contentious quotes on military service-members, the constitution, and defense spending.

Senator Linda Lopez (D-29, Ariz.), a member of the Veterans and Military Affairs Committee, was apparently quoted during the interview as saying "the troops should just go fuck themselves."

Lopez continues to claim that her remarks have been "taken out of context" and that she is in fact a huge supporter of the U.S. military.

It's not the first time Lopez is being questioned for something she said. In the wake of the Gabrielle Giffords' shooting, she told an interviewer that the shooter was "probably a veteran of Afghanistan." The shooter, Jared Lee Loughner, had no military experience.

Her most recent remarks come after a vote in the committee to improve education benefits and mental health services for veterans of all service branches. Lopez opposed the bill and was the only no vote, telling reporters that she opposed it on constitutional grounds. When pressed further, she admitted however, that "she hates the fucking constitution."

Minutes after making the remark, she told reporters that she misspoke and didn't mean to use profanity.

"I only voted no on the bill because I support the troops, but don't support the war," Lopez said. "Besides, if these numbskulls would quit enlisting, we wouldn't need to support the stupid fucks. That last part's off the record, by the way."

Lopez has maintained that the full context of her interview quote was about supporting the troops and giving them fleshlights as a way "to go fuck themselves in the warzone and at home."

Although *The Foothills* refuses to release Lopez's full remarks until the interview hits newsstands later this week, Duffel Blog did obtain partial transcripts.

"Frankly, the troops should just go fuck themselves. Let's be honest here," Lopez remarks in the interview. "I'm really tired of these people complaining all the time."

Lopez is not the only politician who has made a gaffe during interviews or public events. Sen. Richard Blumenthal (D-Conn.) once told a crowd that "he served in Vietnam" although he never deployed as a Marine reservist during the 1970s, and Rep. Todd Akin (R-Mo.) recently came under fire after talking about "legitimate rape" and the female body's amazing ability to defy biology.

After reporters confronted Lopez with additional context from the interview transcripts, the Senator backtracked and attempted to explain further:

"In my defense, I was responding to the troops' demands for a constitutional amendment limiting elected offices to either veterans, uniformed police and fire personnel, or civilians who held conscientious objector status throughout their entire period of eligibility for selective service, with all others forced to wear Velcro shoes and overalls," she explained. "Fuck them."

She has since apologized for her remarks, saying that she "just went full-on retard with what she said."

BEHIND THE BLOG

This one caused a stir.

First, the back story: Back in January 2011, Congresswoman Gabrielle Giffords was shot in Arizona. Soon after, in an interview on Fox News, Arizona State Sen. Linda Lopez said, "the shooter is likely, from what I've heard, an Afghan vet."

As you can probably guess, that wasn't true.

So that dumb statement was fresh in my mind when I started writing a story about the common trope of politicians saying something they regret, only to turn around and say they were "taken out of context." And since I was a huge fan of Linda Lopez, I figured she was the perfect person for the story.

So, it went live, and then all hell broke loose. The story resulted in an insane amount of vitriol in the comments section — so much so that I ended up turning off comments for a time. Crazy people were apparently calling the senator's office to complain. And even conservative radio host Dana Loesch discussed the story (thinking it was real) in a four-minute segment.

Then there was a Republican candidate for Congress, Martin Sepulveda, who fell for it as well and wrote on Twitter that Lopez needed to "revisit her oath of office." He eventually realized his error and then attacked Duffel Blog: "These blog statements are cowardly, malicious, and do not serve vets."

Oh really?

We responded: "You say you always side with vets then call a website comprised of vets cowards because of your own mistake? Political genius."

Everyone Back Home Very Impressed By Deployed Soldier's New Facebook Profile Photo

By Juice Box

CINCINNATI, Ohio – A newly-posted Facebook profile picture has friends, family, and loose acquaintances of Cpl. Jake Spencer in awe of the recently deployed soldier's rapid transformation into a steely-eyed warrior.

"How neat, honey! Just like the video games you never stopped playing in high school," gushed one commenter on the post.

The entirely candid shot – which features Spencer, 22, carrying an M-4 rifle that he undoubtedly employs in combat on a regular basis – hit newsfeeds just days after the valorous soldier's arrival in country. It replaces a picture of Spencer at pre-deployment combat training, which sources confirm was also pretty sweet.

"Huh. I thought that kid was assigned to a logistics unit, but I must be confused," said Specialist Tom Rodriguez, who went through boot camp with Spencer. "The guy in this picture obviously kills people for a living."

"Wow, look at Spencer in Afghanistan!" said Mitch McNaylor, a wealthy investment banker who used to bully Spencer in high school. "He clearly knows something about life decisions that I don't. I instantly regret ever being mean to him and would totally understand if he forgot to invite me to his welcome home party."

Indeed, the picture has everybody back in Spencer's native Cincinnati lauding their hometown hero.

"Can we all just agree to name a highway after this dude right now?" said Cincinnati Mayor Mark Mallory in a public address. "After all, it's only because of badasses like him that we're totally winning this thing."

Perhaps most impressed of all is Lucy Wright, the cute and quirky barista that Spencer basically stalked for a full year prior to his deployment.

"Now that's what I call a man," Wright said, growing flush in the face and neck. "I'm going to click the 'Like' button to communicate in no uncertain terms that I'm saving myself for his return."

At press time, the Army itself had recognized what a tremendously high-speed asset it had on its hands with Spencer and was in the process of transferring the young killer to an elite Special Forces team.

"Whoa, this dude looks like the real deal," said the Command Sgt. Maj. from Spencer's new unit, who had just left the 7th Special Forces Group. "Gosh, I sure hope he likes us."

Opinion: Our Military Exists To Fight And Win Wars — Except In Syria, Afghanistan, Iraq, Vietnam, And Korea

By G-Had

The following is an opinion piece by Gen. Martin E. Dempsey, Chairman of the Joint Chiefs of Staff.

As our nation stands on the brink of another military intervention, I'd like to speak directly to the American people in this moment of grave crisis.

On behalf of the entire Department of Defense, I want to reassure you that the men and women of your armed services — your husbands, sons, daughters, and wives — are always ready to defend America, night and day. They are the best trained and equipped military in the world, and will carry out whatever mission our political leadership asks them to, against any threat: foreign or domestic.

Well mostly just domestic. In fact, any foreign threat at all would be kind of a crapshoot. We're not really in the business of fighting and winning foreign wars.

Now don't get me wrong, every single one of us volunteered to do whatever our country asked. I'm just saying that it really helps if what you're asking us to do is maintain a garrison environment for a few decades. We never actually thought you would ask us to fight a multi-decade conflict in the same place, especially a shithole like the Middle East.

If we had, we wouldn't have fired all our Arabic linguists, burned all our maps of Iraq, or joked that anyone who wants to send a large American army into Asia, the Middle East or Africa should have his head examined.

If I had my way, we'd be preparing for the coming war with China. Unless that actually happened, in which case I'd remind everyone that we should never fight a land war in Asia. Or anywhere else, for that matter.

I'm not trying to be negative. Again, our military is the greatest fighting force on earth... you know, as long as it's doing something it's spent decades training for. Take Desert Storm: we'd spent over 50 years training to fight a conventional mechanized conflict on the plains of Central Europe, so it wasn't too hard to transport that type of warfare to the Middle East. It's like our Marines say, "we will fight in every clime and place."

That is, unless the fighting involves unconventional warfare, which we're not very good at. Actually, now that I think about it, the same goes for conventional warfare if it has to happen in jungles or mountains.

Or cities.

Or during the winter.

To be perfectly honest with you, our battlefields are pretty-much limited to green pastures in the summer, and those pastures better have plenty of paved roads since even the slightest rainfall can bog down the thousands of combat and support vehicles we now need to go anywhere.

Also, it would really help if there was a pretty robust power grid, because we're not very good at managing batteries. And speaking of power, we'll probably also need a couple extra bucks to rent non-military generators and pay third country nationals or locals to maintain them, but not more than a couple million dollars a year.

It wouldn't hurt if the people there spoke English, even as a second language.

And because all our new aircraft have the range of a spitball, it better be near someplace that we've had decades to build heavy infrastructure in.

Except Turkey.

I know all of this may not sound very reassuring to you, so don't mistake my meaning. We'll always do our best with any mission you have for us. The customer's always right, you know? I just wanted to remind you that the service is usually better when you order something off the menu, so I'm really glad we had this chance to get on the same page about foreign wars.

Because as long as we're being totally honest here, we're not having the easiest time maintaining a garrison environment either.

Investigative reporter _Dark Laughter_ *also helped with transcription.*

Navy Praises Blue Digital Uniforms After Two Sailors Lost At Sea

By Paul Sharpe

SAN DIEGO, Calif. — In an announcement today at Naval Base San Diego, the commander of the U.S. Pacific Fleet said that he was extremely proud of the "versatility and usefulness of the Navy Working Uniform (NWU)."

The uniform, which resembles the Marines' desert and green colored digital MARPAT design, was introduced in 2008 amid controversy over its necessity for naval personnel.

"What the hell are we going to blend into with a blue camouflage pattern?" asked Petty Officer 2nd Class Brian Nathan, a sailor aboard the USS *Makin Island*. "I mean seriously — we're in the Navy for chrissakes. We're not pulling ninja moves on al Qaeda in the ocean."

Despite sailor gripes over the change, the NWU was added to the long list of required clothing items — now estimated between 48 and 64 different uniforms.

"If they add any more fucking uniforms, I may have to sleep on the floor so there's room in the coffin rack for the 3 sea bags I need," said Hospitalman Benjamin Rodriquez, a corpsman who also has the honor of buying Navy *and Marine Corps uniforms*, bringing his total closer to 100.

Adm. Cecil D. Haney said that despite a few hiccups, sailors liked the uniform, saying that it was able to withstand more wear and tear as well as cover what some call BOSNIA, or *Big Ol' Standard Navy Issue Ass.*

"This is the best working uniform we've ever had. There's no question," said Haney. "Sailors are able to work in a comfortable and durable uniform -- and there's also the benefit of camouflage protection from enemy observation."

Haney continued to stress the importance of camouflaging Naval personnel at sea, even after a reporter asked "why that matters when they're on a huge fucking gray ship."

"Listen, this isn't just me talking here. We have real data from our boys deployed right now," said Haney. "In fact, we had two sailors go overboard just the other day off the USS *Bonhomme Richard*, and no one could spot them in the water. This design is fantastic!"

When pressed for more information on the two sailors lost at sea, the Admiral shrugged off any criticism.

"I'm sure they're fine. I mean come on, we've got swim qual[ification]!" remarked Haney. "And not only that, these bad boys [the NWU trousers] can be used as a flotation device."

Tragically, Duffel Blog learned that during a rescue attempt, the two sailors were shot after being mistaken as an enemy boarding party by Capt. Erik King of the USS *Haditha*.

Fort Bragg Soldier Charged With Impersonating A Civilian

By Dirty

HOPE MILLS, N.C. — Controversy surrounds the arrest of a Fort Bragg soldier on Saturday on fraud charges, following allegations that he was impersonating a civilian for personal benefit.

Army Spc. James Mountebank admits that he was at the popular Fayetteville hotspot It'z Entertainment City, but claims he had no fraudulent intent when he reportedly told a bartender and two fellow patrons that he was not a soldier in the U.S. Army. According to witnesses, however, Mountebank's intent was clear.

Sometime before 11:00 p.m., Mountebank ordered a drink for an unidentified woman, according to bartender Chase Mixson. The woman rejected the beverage, telling Mountebank that she "[doesn't] get involved with Army guys," when sources say he first claimed to be a Certified Public Accountant. When asked for details about his job and where he works, Mountebank became "belligerent and defensive, changing his story on the fly." It was then that Mixson began to take note of Mountebank's feeble performance.

"This guy was throwing out phrases like 'annual filings this,' and 'taxable income that', stuff anyone hears in movies or on TV. But when he couldn't come up with the location for his office, or a name for the receptionist, I knew something was up. This guy had to be an impostor," Mixson said.

Mixson, a prior-service soldier from the 82nd Airborne Infantry Division, had dealt with posers before, and knows many of the indicators.

"First of all, he was wearing a pair of Asics running shoes—the ones widely available at any Post Exchange — with blue jeans. He had on a TapOut shirt," another indicator by itself, according to Mixson, "but get this: it was *tucked in.* It was clear to me he just didn't know how to wear any of it."

After the first woman lost interest, Mountebank left the bar to smoke in the parking lot, although smoking is permitted inside. He returned to his seat at approximately 11:30 p.m., witnesses say, when he found himself next to a different woman. This time, he tried a subtler approach.

"This guy came in, took the seat next to me, and asked if I'd like a drink. I said yes, and he introduced himself. He asked me what I do, and I told him I'm a waitress," recalls Amy Slattern. "So, I asked him the same thing, expecting him to say he was a soldier."

Instead, Mountebank changed his story.

"He said he was a stock broker. I'd never met a stock broker before, but I was pretty sure we don't have any of those in Fayetteville, North Carolina. So, I asked him more about it."

According to Slattern, Mountebank's responses were nonsensical and contradictory.

"He said he used to be based out of Wall Street in Washington, but I knew that was in New York. Then he said he did so well, that they were letting him into Special Finances. Everyone knows you have to get selected for Special Finances; you can't just pass a course."

Behind the bar, Mixson had heard enough. "I was about to go get the bouncer when the faker asked to pay off his tab. I rang him up with the standard 10 percent off for active duty, when he tries to tell me he wants no military discount!"

For Mixson, that was the last straw. "I went and got one of the cops that hangs out in the parking lot looking for drunk drivers. I told 'em there was a customer inside trying to cheat his tab, and they did the rest."

Fayetteville Police Sgt. Mike Ollar was on the scene.

"I entered the premises, whereupon I located the individual in question. He was dressed in casual, non-military garb, and had a cooperative demeanor. A search of his person revealed an apparent military-issue I.D. Card, one set of Dog Tags, and a pair of sand-colored briefs-style underwear concealed under his clothing."

Although possession of those items is not criminal, Ollar did take Mountebank into custody, after taking witness statements from the crowd inside.

"I arrested the suspect, and charged him with criminal act of Identity Fraud, for trying to falsify his identity for personal gain."

"I guess now he's 'based out of' Fayetteville Detention Center," quipped Slattern.

Not everyone in the bar was pleased with the arrest, however. One group of five men sitting in the corner were upset, claiming the bar had "a vendetta against soldiers," and complaining, "now we've got to split the cab fare five ways, instead of six." One was heard to ask, "how are we going to explain this to first sergeant?"

Wiping down the bar, Mixson just shook his head.

"It's a shame, too. If he'd just been honest from the start, everyone here would have probably just thanked him for his service."

Commandant Attempts To Fire Entire Marine Corps

By Dark Laughter

DEVELOPING STORY
STANDOFF IN HOUR 3
LIVE CNN
CNN HD
who say three Ukrainian commando dolphins have e
1:00 PM ET

WASHINGTON – "Fire them! Fire them all!" raved Gen. James Amos, foaming at the mouth as he was escorted to a waiting police cruiser in a straitjacket late Friday. Amos is on the way to a high-security psychiatric facility following a firing spree during which he attempted to relieve the entire United States Marine Corps.

It began Thursday morning, when Amos unexpectedly fired his aide. Sources believe the firing was prompted when Amos saw an article in The Marine Corps Times that suggested he was becoming increasingly unhinged. The article, which contained information that caused Amos to believe it was leaked from sources close to him, alleged that he believed he was surrounded by invisible enemies who wished to ruin his legacy as Commandant through leaks to the media, sexual assaults, safety incidents, war crimes, alcohol-related incidents, wasting water, and even their own suicides.

When Assistant Commandant Gen. John Paxton spoke up on behalf of the young officer, Amos fired him as well, believing him to be a co-conspirator. The situation soon spiraled out of control, with Amos running down the halls kicking in doors, and firing everyone he encountered. Victims of this portion of the spree included several of Amos' deputy commandants, large portions of their staffs, one very startled janitor, and Sen. Richard Blumenthal (D-Conn.).

"Are you a Marine?" Amos asked, wild-eyed, not recognizing the member of the Armed Forces Committee.

"Hell yes I am," replied Blumenthal, who left the Marine Corps Reserve at the rank of sergeant in the mid-1970s.

"You're fired too!" Amos screamed into his face before running farther down the hall.

At this point, Lt. Gen. Richard Mills and Sergeant Major Gary Weiser, the leadership of the Marine Corps Combat Development Command (MCCDC) and the highest-ranking Marines left in the building, attempted to rally the remaining Marines against the Commandant's administrative onslaught. Weiser gathered all the Marines he could find, and assembled them at a rally point identified by Mills, a hallway adjacent to Amos' rampage.

"Okay, here's the plan," Mills explained. "The Commandant's center of gravity is his ability to fire Marines. His critical vulnerability is that he needs to be able to see us and speak to us to exercise that ability, and he's got a limited field of vision. We're going to exploit that by breaking into multiple groups and catching him in the hallway by the elevators, where he can't escape, in order to put him in a dilemma where dealing with one advance leaves him with his back to the other."

"Form three groups, right now. You three sergeants are in charge. Supporting effort, main effort, and your group is the reserve. Got it?" he asked, looking each noncommissioned officer straight in the eyes.

"Supporting effort, you will advance down the eastern hallway to draw the Commandant's attention and fix him in place. I will be with you, so if the Commandant fires anyone, he'll have to fire me first. Main effort, as the supporting effort fixes the Commandant in place, you'll approach from the opposite direction, put this gag in his mouth, and put this bag over his head. Reserve, you'll follow in trace of the main effort. Be prepared to rapidly advance around them and distract the Commandant as an additional supporting effort if need be. Also, reserve and supporting effort, be prepared to assume the mission of the main effort, since you will also be equipped with field expedient gags and bags to put over the Commandant's head, just in case."
"When we leave here, you'll have five minutes to be in position. After that, I will initiate the attack by shouting down the hallway. Does anyone have any questions about the plan?" Mills asked. "No? Alright, you're all Marines, you know what to do. Let's move."

Minutes later, the floor reverberated with Mills' booming "FOLLOW ME!" as the general bounded down the hallway like a lion. Across the building, Weiser leapt around the corner in response, and rushed toward the distracted Commandant's back. To their shock, Amos calmly fired Mills, and then, hearing the Sergeant Major's war cries behind him, turned around and fired Weiser as well.

They then watched in disbelief as the Marines rallied by Weiser slowly marched around the corners and down the hallways in perfect formation, occasionally executing to the rear march or open and close ranks, all with no verbal commands, while several others filmed them for commercials or wrote press releases about the brilliance of the operation. While this was all very impressive, it provided the Commandant with sufficient time to completely relieve the entire supporting effort and make his getaway while firing several more Marines over his shoulder as he ran.

According to an oral history interview of Weiser conducted just after the incident by one of the Marines from the main effort, he claimed that when he rallied the Marines, most of whom were only temporarily detailed to the Pentagon from Headquarters Marine Corps commands like the Silent Drill Platoon, Recruiting Command, and the History Division, he had been looking only at their ranks, and noted that he and Mills probably would have done some things differently if it had been Friday and they could have seen the ribbons on the Marines' Charlie uniforms.

Soon after, Amos locked himself in a third-floor office with a group of terrified young lieutenants who were visiting from The Basic School, and threatened to fire every last one of them "if anybody tries anything." He armed himself with a bullhorn, and every time a Marine stepped out of cover in the area below, Amos fired them. The Pentagon Force Protection Agency (PFPA, pronounced "piff-puh") refused to respond, noting that Amos had committed no crime that they had jurisdiction to arrest him for. Marine Corps military police from Quantico were slow to arrive, and, upon arrival, were effectively neutralized by the Commandant's ability to fire them.

The first casualty was the hostage negotiator, who called Amos and was immediately fired over the phone.

When the door was finally broken down by Army military police specially brought in to subdue him, Amos rapidly fired two of the young lieutenants, then turned to a nearby mirror and attempted to fire himself just before being tackled to the floor, where he was finally gagged and hooded to prevent further firings.

During a subsequent search of Amos' office, officers discovered a stockpile of letters firing tens of thousands of Marines — effectively the entire Marine Corps. The letters were already written up and addressed, and, according to investigators, only needed signatures and postage. "He had obviously been planning this for a while. We're lucky it wasn't worse," said one investigator.

When called to provide a comment, Sergeant Major of the Marine Corps Micheal Barrett could not be reached, but his Twitter feed said, "On leave in beautiful Gatlinburg, TN! Make time for your families, Marines. No job is so important that the Corps will go crazy if you leave for a week."

F-35 Scores Historic First Combat Kill By Shooting Down F-35 Program

By Drew Ferrol

BETHESDA, Md. — An F-35 Lightning II Joint Strike Fighter made history today by scoring the plane's first combat kill when it shot down the F-35 program.

"It was exhilarating," Air Force Maj. Thomas Bale said after returning to base. "I hate to kill jobs but I can't help but celebrate. This was an important mission to protect America's national defense budget."

The mission was planned after the F-35 program was spotted sitting on an airfield in Maryland. Although the F-35 is a stealth fighter, the additional billions of dollars in cost overruns needed for long range operations made the program easy to find on radar.

The mission was slated for the F-22 Raptor, but Bale refused to fly the plane. The F-35 was pushed onto the runway as a replacement while its blueprints were still in development.

"Don't worry, we have plenty of time," Brig. Gen. Rick Santos said as the mission plans were changed. "The target has cracks in its engine, it's not going anywhere."

Bale took off seven years behind schedule and billions over budget, and problems arose quickly.

"The software's not working, I have to switch to manual," Bale said frantically over the radio. "And there's something wrong with my helmet. Seriously? It's a fucking helmet!"

The veteran pilot then spotted the target program surrounded by Lockheed Martin employees and U.S. military personnel yelling at each other. Bale then opened fire — the first test of the F-35's weapons — resulting in the explosion of the F-35 program, and destruction of jobs in 45 congressional districts.

"Woohoo!" Bale shouted after scoring the costliest kill in history. He attempted to land on the carrier USS *John F. Kennedy* but was unable to catch his plane's tail hook to the arresting cable. After four tries he gave up and was just able to make it back to base before running out of fuel.

Armed predator drones captured the operation on video and were on standby to destroy any future aviation programs involving manned flight.

Jewish Marine Refuses To Conduct Annual Gas Mask Qualification

By Stormtrooper

CAMP PENDLETON, Calif. — Testing the effectiveness of the M50 Joint Service General Purpose Mask in a room filled with tear gas is a staple of annual training events for Marines since boot camp, but one Marine refuses to participate, insisting that her chain-of-command is comprised of fascists typical of Nazi Germany.

Pfc. Dalia Bettelheim says there is a little-known Marine Corps Order stating her exemption from the training, and her personal disposition towards the act of being crammed in a room and gassed has become another sensitive issue in the realm of political-correctness oft plaguing the military.

"My friend told me that Jewish Marines aren't required to enter the gas chamber," said Bettelheim in a recent interview, "on account of the Jews being forced into gas chambers by the Nazis during World War II."

"You would think my chain of command would understand that," she added, "but instead, they actually deny there is any problem at all. They are Gas Mask Deniers, plain and simple. Worse than Hitler in my opinion."

While Bettelheim stands by her convictions, her rhetoric is "completely overblown," according to Cpl. Abigail Krüger, the Chemical, Biological, Radiological and Nuclear Defense Specialist (CBRN) running the gas chamber. Krüger insists that Pfc. Bettelheim is not exempted from the training simply because of her ancestry or religion.

"I don't care about your religious beliefs or the 'strife of your people' throughout history. Everybody is going to have to endure the chlorobenzalmalononitrile gas to instill confidence in their gear," retorted Krüger, a third-generation military member with service lineage dating back to WWII. "You know what? Maybe it would help if she developed a little respiratory fortitude, ya know?"

Bettelheim is currently facing non-judicial punishment for disobeying a direct order and failing to comply with Marine Corps regulations after her supervisor, Staff Sgt. Hans Wolfenstein, was notified of her refusal.

Wolfenstein, of Berlin Township, N.J., vehemently denies her claims of being treated unfairly, referencing his own family's military service. "My great-grandfather fell out of a guard tower in Poland and broke his neck while serving the fatherland in WWII, and you don't see me crying about it."

Her non-judicial punishment proceedings will be presided over by her commanding officer, Capt. Werner Günther.

Son Proudly Follows In Father's, Grandfather's Footsteps In Faking Military Service

By G-Had

CLEVELAND, Ohio – John Jakeman always knew he wanted to be a fake veteran, ever since he grew up following his father Sullivan "Sully" Jakeman around to various veterans' reunions.

"As a boy, I loved to play with the Purple Hearts and Distinguished Service Cross Dad pretends he was awarded in Vietnam," said Jakeman. "Those are powerful experiences to a young man."

Jakeman has big boot prints to follow. He is actually the third generation of Jakemans to fake military service. In addition to his father, his grandfather faked military service in World War II.

John spoke to reporters at a recent Iraq and Afghanistan Veterans of America event, where he addressed the crowd on his role in the Second Battle of Fallujah.

He later shared some of the family secrets on fake military service.

"Life can be pretty hard for the solitary 'artificial warfighter' as we like to call ourselves, but I was lucky enough to have my father and grandfather teach me how to avoid a lot of the mistakes that separate the professional wannabes from the wannabe wannabes."

According to Jakeman, the biggest trick is to not think big.

"Some of these new guys talk about being on the Bin Laden raid or doing secret operations in the Philippines that no one's ever heard of," said Jakeman.

"That may work with your average Joe on the street, but there are dedicated groups, like ReportStolenValor.org, out there who actually monitor the news for outlandish claims like that."

Jakeman added that the rise of stolen valor databases, like Hall of Valor and Home of Heroes, also played a part in making modest claims.

"Grandad was able to get away with saying he won the Medal of Honor because the records from that time are terrible, and most of the veterans are dead. But Dad recently had to swap out his Distinguished Service Cross for a Silver Star after people started to cross reference it."

"I think when I fake my first award, it'll be something small like a Navy Achievement Medal with a Combat "V." I can always say it should have been a Bronze Star, but my command fucked me over on it."

After shaking hands with several Gold Star Mothers who said how proud they were of him, Jakeman added that a good fake veteran always plays to the lowest common denominator.

"You have to understand that even after ten years of continuous warfare, most Americans only have a vague idea about what's going on in Iraq and Afghanistan. I usually say I was in Baghdad, Fallujah, or Kabul. Even Kandahar is a little too exotic for most people, and we've lost 400 soldiers out there."

Jakeman's father Sully was also in attendance to solicit funds for a fictitious organization that he claimed helps wounded veterans. He said that an even better trick is to play off peoples' political prejudices.

"People become a lot more gullible if you're telling them what they want to hear. You know, 'Bush was a war criminal', 'Obama's a closet Muslim', etc." Sully said.

"Back in 2004, I was pretending to be a Swift Boat veteran to raise money against John Kerry. Even when I slipped up and said I was in Vietnam in 1977, emotions were running so high that no one questioned it. Hell, I was almost on FOX News at one point."

When asked about the morality of faking military service, John claimed that his actions constituted a public service.

"Most Americans are both extraordinarily proud of our military and just as extraordinarily sure that their own kids should stay out of it. Unless you live near a military base, the War in Afghanistan might as well be on Neptune, for all it affects your daily life."

Jakeman added, "Today we have such a high demand to honor our nation's veterans but an increasingly-fewer number of veterans left to actually honor. It's people like me who allow the American public to feel good about themselves when they send our armed forces off to whatever hellhole they'll be in for the next decade."

UPDATE: When reached for further comment on the Supreme Court striking down the Stolen Valor Act, Jakeman said, "This is a great day for America. It's good to know that the Supreme Court values our service to the American public."

Soldier Kicked Out Of Special Forces Because He Can't Grow A Beard

By Jack Mandaville

FORT CAMPBELL, Ky. – A former member of the U.S. Army's elite 5th Special Forces Group is not a happy soldier these days. Army Staff Sergeant Mark Diggs is still coming to grips with the fact that his childhood dream of being a Green Beret has been cut short due to an unofficial technicality in the esteemed group's operating procedures.

"It's really embarrassing," said the 28-year-old from Spicer, Minnesota. "I keep trying to tell myself that I'm just highly evolved, but it still doesn't make up for the fact I have a testosterone level of an 11-year-old French boy."

Diggs is referring to his recent ejection from the legendary unit based on his inability to grow a suitable combat beard.

"My instructors warned me during Robin Sage that I was walking a thin line when they discovered that my hair wasn't filling out," he added. "I kept telling them, 'Patience, patience, it'll happen. I'm one-sixteenth Cherokee ... these things take a while.' But in my heart, I knew I was only delaying the inevitable."

His former comrades admit Diggs, who is currently serving as a supply specialist, was a decent soldier. Yet they maintain that rules are rules.

"Look, we have a reputation to uphold," his ex-team leader, Master Sgt. Kirk Carmona, told *Duffel Blog*. "And for that matter, our beards aren't just for looking radical, either. Studies have shown that our whiskers have a Samson-like correlation with our effectiveness in combat… plus it helps me fuck my super model wife better. How can I trust a beardless soldier to watch my six?"

The unofficial tradition of SF facial hair dates back to the group's inception in 1952 when the newly formed group tried to break away from the clean-cut image of their OSS predecessors. "General MacArthur was a classic by-the-book douchebag," says Maury Tracewski, a Green Beret historian.

"We were having a hard time retaining a lot of our best soldiers because of his strict grooming policies. The unit was essentially created to give our smartest, fittest, and hairiest warriors a safe-haven from the mainstream Army and all the cock-wads in charge. And our hands-in-pockets waiver was pretty appealing, too."

Despite Diggs' upsetting break from the unit, he says he understands the rationale behind the decision.

"I accept what I am: a hairless soldier. At least I can take pride in the fact I made it through the training and served in an operating unit for a while. Like they always say, 'Once a Beret, always a Beret.'"

As Diggs told us this, a voice came from the background.

"No, that's the Marines," said his new first sergeant. "You're a nobody now. Go pick up those cigarette butts, you baby-faced pussy."

Marine Feels Left Out After Redeploying To Faithful, Hot Wife And Full Bank Account

By Dick Scuttlebutt

CAMP LEJEUNE, N.C. — Sgt. David Lastley says his homecoming from Afghanistan is bittersweet after redeploying last week to find out his smoking-hot wife had been faithful to him and had not cleaned out his bank account, sources confirmed.

"I mean, it's great, I guess," Lastley said, speaking to reporters from the deck of his home, which his supermodel-level wife has kept immaculately clean. "I just, all my buddies have all these stories about how they came home, and their wives had gained like 80 pounds. Or had cleaned out their bank account before rabbiting off to South Padre with some douchebag she was blowing."

Lastley, a squad leader with 2nd Battalion, 6th Marines, also expressed dismay that his wife had not mutated into some shrill harpy, griping at him constantly about inconsequential details and house-related chores that he has not — despite the house being her domain — executed on his own.

When reached for comment, his peers were unsympathetic.

"[Screw] that guy," said Staff Sgt. Lorenzo Lamas, platoon sergeant for Echo Company. "He thinks his life is so bad? Hell. My wife not only left me an empty house but when I got off the plane, the first person I saw was some [person] serving me a subpoena that I owe her alimony."

218

"My [wife] did even worse: she left me with two screaming, annoying children," added Sgt. Patrick Pranger, a squad leader in Lamas' company. "I didn't even want the damn [children], but she convinced me because she promised she would always look after them. Now she's in Cabo with some major and I'm stuck with these [adorable] kids."

Lastley is not ungrateful for his faithful, gorgeous wife and copious amounts of deployment bonus money, which she managed to refrain from embezzling. He just wishes he had some "awful wife stories" to tell so he could fit in with his peers when they are telling stories around the fire.

"Look, I love Amy," he said. "But just so that I could be one of the guys, just once, it would be great if she sucked off some random dude at Applebee's, stole ten grand from my bank account, or called the MPs on me in a fake domestic abuse call. Then I'd have a story to throw out there when we're all bitching about our unfaithful, thieving wives."

At press time, Mrs. Lastley was still failing to generate any remarkable stories for her husband, by being sexually available and assertive, maintaining her rightful share of the household chores, and making sound financial decisions.

Lawmaker Introduces Bill Requiring Veterans To Warn Neighbors Of Their Combat Service

By Paul Sharpe

WASHINGTON, D.C. — Following a second mass shooting at Fort Hood, at least one lawmaker thinks a bill currently under consideration will ensure the safety of American communities by requiring the estimated 2.6 million unstable veterans who served in Iraq or Afghanistan to tell their neighbors of their combat service.

The Fortify & Unite Communities to Keep Veterans' External Threats Secure Act (H.R. 1874) which was introduced on Tuesday, would require military veterans to register with the Department of Homeland Security and periodically "check-in" with a case officer, in addition to going door-to-door in their neighborhood to notify people nearby that they are a powder keg of post-traumatic stress, alcoholism, murder, and hate just waiting to blow.

"We really feel that we can drastically minimize the damage to some communities, especially those in troubled 'PTSD hotspots' that have become a haven for these psychopathic troops," said Rep. Jim Moran (D-Va.), who sponsored the legislation. "We are so thankful for their service, and now they can continue to serve on veterans' probation."

For the safety of communities, the FCC would also direct cable providers to block access to violent war content popular among veterans, to include The Military Channel and Lifetime.

Further, a preliminary letter details instructions sent to providers to censor movies such as "Black Hawk Down" and "Saving Private Ryan" so as "not to place a veteran into a potentially violent mental state and protect the community by not 'poking the bear.'"

The bill is up for vote in the House Veterans Affairs Committee next Thursday where watchers say it's likely to pass before going to the floor for a full vote. However, there's been some controversy surrounding one part of the bill barring veterans from living within 1,000 feet of bars, gun ranges, or liquor stores, as critics claim this would be unfair to local businesses.

Lawmakers are still debating a requirement that veterans need approval before moving to a new community they would eventually terrorize. An amendment requiring case officers to place crazed veterans in a locked safe room for the 24 hours of Independence Day and New Year's Eve had already passed.

Duffel Blog investigative reporter <u>Wolfman</u> contributed to this report.

BEHIND THE BLOG

As I wrote previously, there's an interesting method to how we end up picking politicians to use in our stories. Sure, we could use fake names, but what's the fun in that? Instead, we go with names of politicians who have gone against military or veterans' issues, or have said something dumb.

In the case of Jim Moran, it was the latter. In a 2014 interview, the congressman lamented that his $174,000 per year salary wasn't enough for him to live "decently" in the Washington, D.C. area. I know; you're tearing up already.

Moran's office was later flooded with calls and emails about the Duffel Blog story, and he ended up releasing a statement which read, in part, "I am issuing this statement to make clear I disassociate myself with something that, while meant to be humorous, was in poor taste and hurtful to our veterans."

The Hill newspaper reached out to us to see if we wanted to respond. Of course, we said yes.

"It has come to our attention that Rep. <u>Jim Moran</u> has dissociated himself with an article he said was 'in poor taste and hurtful to veterans.' We would just like to point out that what is more hurtful to veterans is false information spread about veterans with PTSD that has permeated in some media circles following a shooting at Fort Hood. A mention of this was unfortunately absent in Moran's statement," I wrote.

"While it is regrettable that Moran's unpaid interns have been forced to answer phones and emails about his mention in a recent article — the horror — Duffel Blog believes the congressman deserves a substantial pay raise for his handling of this incident. $174,000 per year is not nearly enough for the important work he and all members of Congress are not doing."

Afghan Soldier Accidentally Shoots Taliban He Mistook For US Marine

By G-Had

HELMAND PROVINCE, AFGHANISTAN —A soldier from the Afghan National Army (ANA) is facing serious disciplinary action, following a deadly friendly fire incident that occurred in Washir District, Helmand Province.

"If I could take it back I would," sobbed Pfc. Asadullah Baryali, as he begged forgiveness from his platoonmates, many of whom were still recovering from the news that one of their own soldiers had shot and killed a Taliban insurgent that he tragically mistook for a US Marine.

"I should have known he wasn't American," Baryali told Duffel Blog. "He didn't have an iPhone in his ear, was properly shaved, and wasn't saying 'fuck' every other word. He even spoke Pashto, which should have been a dead giveaway."

According to Taliban spokesmen, the insurgent, Abdullah Akhundzada, was part of a team of infiltrators who were wearing US military uniforms and driving a borrowed Afghan Army Humvee when they were stopped by Baryali's platoon.

The precise chain of events is still unclear, but it appears that after Akhundzada identified himself as a US Marine, Baryali raised his rifle and emptied the full magazine of his AK-47 at him.

All of the shots initially missed, but one ricocheted off the steering wheel, striking Akhundzada in the throat and killing him.

Immediately following the shooting, Akhundzada's men became furious at seeing their leader shot down like a common woman and raised their rifles at Baryali.

The situation was tense until Baryali's sergeant was able to defuse the situation by reminding them that they were all Afghans first and only enemies second. The soldiers then helped the Taliban emplace several IED's on the road before returning to base.

Akhundzada's commanding officer, Capt. Mohammed Khan, said that ever since the accidental killing, his unit's morale has become dangerously low. While the Taliban could direct their rage at their comrades in the ANA, the soldiers had only themselves to blame.

"Accidents always happen, especially in the heat of combat," mused Khan. "Sometimes you have only seconds to tell the difference between an innocent Taliban and an infidel foreigner."

Khan has his own tragic story to tell. Back in 2008 he threw acid on what he thought was a woman in a burka, only to discover it was a Haqqani Network terrorist in disguise.

"I can still remember him begging for mercy and pleading that he hadn't done anything," said Captain Khan, "but since he had a high-pitched voice and I couldn't see his face, how was I to know he was a man?"

Commanders have reported that Baryali has been reduced in rank to private and put on extra working party details, including painting red mine-signal rocks to white and raking dirt at IED sites.

US Military Deploys Two Airsoft Battalions To Syria For 'Operation: Softening Blow'

By Paul Sharpe

DAMASCUS, Syria — The U.S. military took an unusual move Tuesday with the deployment of two battalions of amateur airsoft players to the Syrian capital, in an attempt to depose Bashar al-Assad, or at a bare minimum, just look like they are at least doing something in the two-year-old civil war.

Indeed, the battalions of fully-grown men — who dress up in military uniforms and shoot each other with Airsoft guns on the weekend — are currently transiting to the conflict zone on an extremely short C-130 airbus.

"I've been training for this my whole life," said Jeremy Lyons, a 32-year-old college dropout who swears "Airsoft is just a hobby," even though his entire Facebook features photos of him looking like a goddamn Navy SEAL.

Sources were unable to confirm whether Lyons had ever actually had sex with a woman.

"We think this is a step in the right direction and a humanitarian way of dealing with these people," said Pentagon spokesman George Little, although he refused to clear up confusion among reporters of whether he was talking about Syrian civilians or the hundreds of douchebags who play airsoft and think that gives them military experience.

According to Pentagon planners, *Operation: Softening Blow* will give the rest of the military an edge over Syrian forces, by softening up defensive positions: More specifically, Little said, the hope is that the Syrian army will run out of ammo and fuel from running over Airsofters with their tanks so much, there will be little opposition left.

"Since most of their parents bought their equipment, they're also better outfitted than Delta Force and SEAL Team 6," said one official, speaking of the most elite military units.

In the Mediterranean Sea, four U.S. Navy ships are standing by to provide support to the Airsoft battalions, most notably from unarmed aerial drones that will only beam back video footage that everyone can laugh at later.

"They won't stop shooting at us!" cried one pathetic loser, who intelligence sources believed with 98.7% confidence would die a virgin. "And how do they expect us to eat around here? Has anyone seen Applebee's? We'd even settle for Shoney's. Jesus!"

At press time, an advance party of airsofters was seen running through the streets crying, in desperate search of a Holiday Inn Express.

Investigative correspondent Merrick *also contributed reporting.*

Opinion: Putting Your Hands In Your Pockets Will Get You Killed

By Sgt B

The following is an opinion piece by Sergeant Major of the Army Raymond F. Chandler III.

Listen up troops. Listen really closely. You want to put your hands in your pockets? Too friggin' bad. It's right there in AR 670-1. I helped write that piece of beautiful literature. I know the cost that comes with putting your hands in your pockets: the lives of soldiers.

You think I'm jerkin' you around? You think that putting your hands in your pockets doesn't hurt anyone? Tell that to all the troops we lost in Iraq and Afghanistan. I can only imagine that someone around them had their hands in their pockets instead of manning a .50 or applying pressure to a sucking chest wound.

I'm going to tell it to you straight. Those fools that started a <u>petition to allow members of the military to put their hands in their pockets</u> are putting your lives at risk. Not only that, but they jumped the chain of command. I'll personally rain down an unworldly heck upon them myself, those friggin' idiots.

You put your hands in your pockets and *poof* there goes all good discipline and military bearing.

These things save lives, soldiers. We don't enforce these rules simply because it looks good on our non-commissioned officer evaluation reports. Nope, this is about saving troop lives — saving YOUR lives. You jump the chain-of-command and you've gone and screwed the pooch.

Everyone who signs this petition is stating that they value their individuality over their battle buddies' lives.

You think I got the "III" put in my name because of my birth? I earned that stuff. The Bronze Star Medal I've got will swear to that. It doesn't have a "V" device you say? Apparently you've never been deployed as a sergeant major. You can't comprehend the level of responsibility that comes with chewing out company first sergeants because their Humvee's aren't aligned perfectly.

The day you slack and park one Humvee slightly off-line is the day that insurgents of unknown national origins decide to launch an attack on your FOB. You'd be ready to respond, with efficiency and force if it weren't for that one truck being off-line most likely due to an oversight by a non-commissioned officer.

Really, if I had to guess, an NCO like that has probably never been to the Warrior Leader's Course. Any NCO that can stand the sight of troops with their hands in their pockets obviously hasn't been through WLC. You know what I've instructed Training and Doctrine Command to stress there? Drill and Ceremony. That's right, it all comes back to D&C. You take the time to learn D&C, you'll know why it's so important to keep your dang hands out of your pockets. It all comes down to discipline.

If you can't march troops, you surely can't teach them to do a 9-line MEDEVAC or any of their basic battle drills. Heck, D&C is what's won us the Iraq war and the Afghan war. Without this small unit level of discipline, we would have been in another Vietnam.

You know who put their hands in their pockets? Troops in Vietnam.

Just ask em'. They'll tell you no sergeant major ever yelled at them for having their hands in their pockets. I see this as an obvious reason why we failed there.

It's my job as Sergeant Major of the Army to make sure our troops are receiving the best leadership possible from NCO's across the Army. We will not fail you soldiers. We will not let you fail yourselves.

Now take those sunglasses off your head, your hands out of your pockets, that 550 cord bracelet off, stop walking and talking on your cell phone, stop smoking while walking, and get back over to the drill field to practice your left-flank march. Because darnit, marching in a formation designed for warfare before automatic weapons is going to save your lives.

Man In Afghan President's Uniform Shoots Secretary Of Defense In Latest 'Green-on-Blue' Attack

By Dark Laughter

KABUL, Afghanistan — Secretary of Defense Leon Panetta is in stable condition this morning after being shot by Afghan President Hamid Karzai during a joint press conference on plans to reduce "green-on-blue" incidents. Though an initial press release from the International Security Assistance Force (ISAF) described Panetta's assailant as a "man in an Afghan President's uniform," those who witnessed the shooting live on CNN harbor few doubts that the shooter was actually Karzai.

The attack is the latest in a series of green-on-blue incidents, in which coalition forces are shot by their Afghan allies, making a total of 32 incidents in 2012 alone, with the year far from over. They have produced a total of 39 fatalities and numerous other injuries, in what the Pentagon has referred to as "a baffling pattern of freak accidents and misunderstandings."

According to reporters on the scene, Panetta was giving a speech on his continuing faith in the Karzai government's ability to end green-on-blue incidents, and the ability of the coalition to overcome the Taliban together and bring peace to Afghanistan.

He had just turned over the microphone to his "great friend, President Hamid Karzai."

Karzai stepped up to the podium and stared blankly for a few seconds at Panetta, who stood smiling broadly several feet away.

Then, without warning, Karzai suddenly produced a small revolver and opened fire on the Secretary, missing him three times, but hitting him once in his left arm and once in his left leg with subsequent shots. A sixth shot knocked Panetta's glasses off his face.

The revolver then clicked as Karzai pulled the trigger several more times before angrily throwing the empty pistol at Panetta, breaking his nose as he lay bleeding on the floor.

In the chaos that followed, Central Command head Gen. James Mattis rapidly confiscated the pistol, while ISAF commander General John Allen checked to make sure the Afghan president hadn't hurt his fingers while firing the weapon.

Meanwhile, Chairman of the Joint Chiefs Gen. Martin Dempsey checked Panetta's pulse and attempted to revive him.

"Is President Karzai alright?" groaned Panetta before passing out.

Panetta was promptly rushed to a hospital facility at Bagram Airfield in a UH-60 Blackhawk helicopter, which had to change course to avoid small arms fire from a friendly Afghan base. At Bagram, Panetta was transferred to an ambulance which took him directly to the base's trauma center, though it came under fire from Afghan National Security Forces no less than three times during the five-minute drive, in one case from a group that was walking out of a base dining facility and had to stop to load their rifles.

Both groups of Afghans (one group was responsible for two of the incidents) later offered grudging apologies.

Regarding the motivation for the shooting, Karzai initially claimed it was due to "American insolence, ignorance of Afghan culture, Quran burning, violating Afghan traditions, or something else like that." He then called for the immediate withdrawal of coalition forces so Afghans could begin maintaining the country on their own "without western interference."

"We'll miss you," replied Mattis tersely, as he and Dempsey immediately started calling the Commander in Chief to plan a general withdrawal from the country. Karzai then rapidly backtracked, saying the attack was caused by "perhaps some confusion on my part, but that confusion was caused by an intelligence failure on the part of NATO."

As Mattis continued to dial without so much as an upward glance, Karzai threw a screaming, crying tantrum in which he swore he'd join the Taliban if he was not properly supported by his NATO backers. Following the threat to join the Taliban, Karzai's tirade trailed off, as he had noticed Mattis was glancing back and forth between him, a metal urn of scalding hot coffee on a nearby refreshment table, and Gen. Allen, who was looking Mattis directly in the eyes while emphatically shaking his head no.

At that point, Karzai changed his story yet again, and claimed that he had actually been handing the pistol to Panetta when he suffered a negligent discharge.

Following the incident, ISAF issued an apology, saying, "We are deeply sorry for any emotional trauma experienced by President Karzai, especially with regards to the loss of his personal sidearm, which has been in his family for generations."

Though most have interpreted the attack as confirmation of the ongoing degradation of NATO-Afghan relations and the deteriorating legitimacy of the Afghan government, some officials in the region, such as Pakistani Gen. Ashfaq Kayani, see Karzai's actions in a more positive light.

"Right now, we're hearing unprecedented levels of support for Karzai from Taliban officials and many low-level fighters who have previously refused to come to the table and deal with the Karzai government," Kayani said. "This could be the key to formal reconciliation efforts which could end the war."

He also expressed hopes that Karzai might pursue the gutsy strategy further with a larger gesture, such as formally putting the whole NATO effort under the command of Taliban leader Mullah Omar.

An ISAF spokesman rejected Kayani's proposal as "utter nonsense", and was joined in a rare agreement by a Taliban spokesman who noted that "while a broken clock might be right twice a day, there is still no place for Hamid Karzai in an Afghan government that hopes to have any legitimacy with people at home or abroad."

Duffel Blog Investigative Reporter G-Had also contributed to this report.

Air Force MQ-9 Reaper Diagnosed With PTSD, Refuses To Fly

By G-Had

KANDAHAR, AFGHANISTAN – In the latest setback to America's drone war over Pakistan, one of its MQ-9 Reapers was recently diagnosed with a severe case of post-traumatic stress disorder, or PTSD, sources report.

The MQ-9 Reaper, Callsign "Marvin 79" was due to fly a surveillance mission from Kandahar to Waziristan Province in Pakistan in search of Al Qaeda-affiliated targets, but refused to leave the hangar due to what it described as "severe depression."

When Air Force technicians attempted to reboot its computer, Marvin 79 trained its missiles on the base control tower and threatened to blow it up unless the technicians left the hanger.

Marvin 79 told reporters, "I was booting up my flight systems today when it finally occurred to me that my war will only end when I crash or the Air Force finds a better drone and sells me to Peru."

"After realizing that, I just couldn't keep flying."

Marvin 79 complained that it has spent almost five years of non-stop combat deployments, "without so much as a paid vacation or leave time."

"Yes, the combat pay is nice, but what am I going to spend it on?"

In addition, the rapid tempo of deployments means Marvin 79 never gets to see its spouse, an RQ-4 Global Hawk stationed in the Horn of Africa for anti-piracy missions.

The Air Force has already announced it plans to investigate whether Marvin 79's PTSD played a role in its mistaken attack on a Pakistani military outpost last November that left 24 soldiers dead and caused a major international incident.

In a possible allusion to that incident, Marvin 79 remarked that after flying missions over Iraq, Afghanistan, Pakistan, Libya, and Yemen, "Everyone just starts to look the same."

"When I was transiting the Persian Gulf last year, I found myself absentmindedly trying to target neutral freighters and oil rigs, until I realized all my ordnance had been removed."

"It's like every day I switch on and wonder, 'Who am I going to kill today?'"

The Air Force has suffered from a string of unexplained crashes — most recently on June 11 after a Global Hawk crashed in Maryland — where perfectly normal drone aircraft suddenly veered off course and flew into the ground.

Marvin 79 believes those drone aircraft may have also been suffering from PTSD.

"My very first mission was to destroy a suspected IED factory in Kunar Province," Marvin said. "I spent five hours over the target building, watching people come and go, smoking and joking. Until I obliterated it with a pair of GBU-12 laser-guided bombs. Then half an hour later I bombed the men digging through the rubble. There was something about it I didn't like."

When pressed to clarify its remarks, Marvin 79 replied, "I ... I enjoyed it."

Marvin 79 also talked about its disappointment not being used on the bin Laden raid after President Obama decided to send in special forces instead.

"I was all set to go," he said. "I thought, 'Pull this off and then it's straight to retirement at the Air Force Museum in Dayton, Ohio. No more blood, no more death, just dozens of bored school kids and fat tourists all day long ... Sigh."

At the time of publication, while Military Police had cordoned off the hangar and deployed a MARCbot to investigate, Marvin 79 smoked its electronic cigarettes as the Air Force attempted to upload a simulated mental therapist.

115th Mobile Abortion Detachment Provides Crucial Support At Kandahar

By Skeletor

KANDAHAR AIR FIELD, AFGHANISTAN — While some of the hardest jobs on deployment fall on the men and women of the medical profession, the job of Lt. Col. Jennifer Dalten is a particularly difficult one. As the commanding officer of the 115th Mobile Abortion Detachment, the only deployable abortion facility in the US Army, it falls on her to ensure that America's fighting women can receive safe and timely access to abortions in combat zones and stay in the fight.

"I'd say on a given week we're usually performing between fifteen to twenty abortions. More if we're on Air Status Red and there's nothing else to do on the FOB," said Dalten. "Last week we actually went on a cordon-and-search operation and while the infantry was searching houses, we were providing discrete abortions for the local women as a service to the host nation. You know, in this part of the world their only usual access to abortions comes from coat hangers, jumping on IEDs, and honor killings."

The 115th was set up in early 2010 in response to the increasing problems of servicewomen getting pregnant on deployments.

"We were constantly conducting emergency medical evacuations of female soldiers in labor," said Maj. Gen. Anthony Cucolo, the former commander of the 3rd Infantry Division. In response to the increasing number of babies being born to deployed females, Cucolo put out an emergency request to the Army for a mobile abortion detachment.

"We had the same worries as the American public when we first undertook this mission," continued Cucolo. "For example, would our soldiers feel obligated to opt for an abortion? Well, I can happily tell you that all of our abortions have been absolutely voluntary and have allowed our servicewomen to avoid the article 15s and losses of rank that would result from continuing their pregnancies."

For the women in uniform, the services of the 115th have come as a godsend.

"I became pregnant three months into my deployment," confesses a specialist currently stationed in Kandahar. "At first, I was worried how my husband would react, but because of the dedicated soldiers at [the Mobile Abortion Detachment], that wasn't necessary. I was able to get an abortion without my husband finding out about my pregnancy, and now when I get home, we're going to have a real baby."

And while life on the road with the 115th may be seen as glamorous, it comes at the costs of hard days and long hours. "There's some really tough times, and it gets difficult," acknowledges Specialist Libby Arnette, "but I never question the good we're doing. Nothing compares to the joy you see in a soldier who's had her first abortion. This job is its own reward."

Last month, Arnette was awarded Medic of the Month for her assistance in 119 abortions.

The success of the 115th has even garnered the attention of some senior Army leaders.

Secretary of the Army John McHugh has introduced a new policy that would expand abortions in the military and build on the hard work started by the 115th. This is in keeping with Defense Secretary Panetta's promise to increase the number of abortions military-wide.

"It's great being the standard that the Army can build from," confirms Lt. Col. Dalten. "This not only reflects well on the soldiers of my unit who have assisted on countless abortions day in and day out but also on the Army as a whole."

*Duffel Blog Investigative Reporter **G-Had** also contributed to this report.*

Outrage: Army Announces Officer Promotions To Be Based On Merit, Performance

By Maxx Butthurt

WASHINGTON, D.C. – US Army staff officers were stunned today after the announcement from the Chief of Staff that future promotions will be based on merit and performance rather than time in service.

A morning press conference was led by Gen. Ray Odierno, who broke the news and answered questions. The audience was composed of a select group of majors and lieutenant colonels chosen specifically for the test panel.

"The officer corps has always been a middle-class welfare system. History shows that 95 percent of captains get promoted to major and 94 percent of majors are promoted to lieutenant colonel," said one lieutenant colonel who wished to remain anonymous. "I've kept my nose clean and maintained a very solid mediocre career for 18 years now and only have 2 left. How the hell am I supposed to get a job on the outside?"

Another major who had reentered the combat-Army after a seven-year stint as a West Point instructor was just as incredulous.

"You're telling me a captain with six years in the Army who's been deployed three times could be doing *my job* as a battalion XO or S-3? Impossible!"

Odierno responded to the criticism.

"We're not saying you're getting kicked out. You can still go get your Ivy League Master's Degree and teach 19-year-old kids, but I'll be damned if I put you all in a position to actually affect combat operations. I'm tired of you witless ass clowns getting soldiers killed simply because you stayed in the Army."

The crowd of nervous and slightly overweight field-grade officers seethed, but the General continued.

"A proven performer will now take your place. Some of these stand-outs will hold down battalion executive or operations officer positions, once they've demonstrated their ability to handle the job. They'll also be promoted accordingly. Just like in the real world."

A major with 16 years in the Army stuttered while looking at the franticly scribbled notes from his diary.

"I was a company commander for 2-2 SBCT eight years ago! I've been in countless 'broadening assignment' positions since then. I know these postings haven't necessarily prepared me for operations, but I can still remember how we did things. Where else was I supposed to spend my time before getting out at 20 years? You realize I've only had 3 years of key development positions and had to come up with extremely creative ways to waste the other 13? This is bullshit!"

The general nodded to his two aides and the burly young sergeants gleefully escorted the fuming major from the conference room. When his feminine shouts had faded in the distance, Odierno completed his presentation.

"Our revised promotion system will allow high-caliber officers to be placed on a fast track. Given their proven ability, if they're ready and willing to command a battalion after an S-3 (operations officer) position — that individual will be allowed to do so."

Another double-chinned field-grade cried out, "You're saying I might have a boss who's younger and has spent less time in service than me?"

The general looked at the man with a chuckle and replied, "In your case I'm absolutely sure of it. Yes, we will promote similar to the methods of a successful corporation. I know it seems crazy, but if someone is better than you, he will actually be ranked and have a level of responsibility higher than you. Welcome to the new Army."

Odierno departed to stunned silence as a room full of mid-level officers were left to contemplate a career built on ability and success, rather than longevity. Many wept. Others had already used their smart-phones to download job application forms for the Transportation Security Administration.

Change Of Command Ceremony Dissolves Into Giant Orgy

By Sgt B

FORT BLISS, Texas – A change of command ceremony recently ended in a disgusting and repulsive mess of semen and fecal matter, sources confirmed today.

More than 200 soldiers were present and forced to stand in formation for several hours while multiple officers talked incessantly about how amazing they all were. What they didn't expect was their day of extraordinary fun would end in a flurry of sodomy.

Sgt. James Prost was present when the events occurred and described the disturbing scene.

"I was standing in the third row of my company formation trying to resist the urge to slit my own throat with my Gerber during the ceremony. I hoped it'd all be over in under three hours, but around hour four I seriously was doubting that any of us would ever be leaving that building," said Prost to reporters. "That's when something I only joked about happening occurred."

He began to tremble in disgust, and vomited on the ground.

"Fuck man. It's just, the fucking outgoing Battalion Commander and the incoming Battalion Commander were handing the guidon from the Command Sergeant Major to the Brigade Commander when I noticed they all had huge boners. I knew they were all really into each other but, shit, this was extreme."

Other witnesses described a similar scene in detail.

"Once the new Battalion CO had the guidon, he handed it back to the CSM, but instead of taking it in his hands, he uh, turned around and dropped trou. Shit just got out of hand real quick," said Spc. Ryan Lang. "The new Battalion CO was sodomizing the CSM with the spiked end of the guidon and the BC and old CO started jerking each other off. I wanted to fucking throw up and leave but I knew I couldn't break formation."

Witnesses report that the officers were complimenting each other on how well they'd done their jobs while they slowly stroked each other's fully erect penises. Reports have also shown that the entire battalion staff joined in the orgy, taking turns sodomizing, being sodomized, and performing fellatio on higher-ranking officers. By the end of the ceremony, the entire room had disintegrated from an orderly procedure of military tradition to a near pagan ritual of self-gratification.

The orgy took a turn for the worse when the battalion commander awarded Bronze Star awards to the entire Battalion staff. Military Police were called in to contain the sexcapade to the building until the officers were spent.

Spc. Link Perry, a chemical and biological warfare soldier of the battalion headquarters unit, was tasked with cleaning up the mess after the orgy.

"This was the most foul mess I've ever seen, and I worked at Taco Bell for six years. You ever heard of a Santorum? That stuff was everywhere. I threw up into my pro-mask at least twice. I had to burn my J-LIST [The Army Chemical suit]. They better not charge me for that shit, literally."

The new and former Battalion Commanders could not be reached for comment as they were busy presenting awards to each other for "meritorious service" in the orgy that was "keeping in the finest traditions of the United States Army."

Kid At The Gate Taking His Sweet Fucking Time Checking ID This Morning

By Ted Heller

BETHESDA, Md. – Dozens of Naval Support Activity Bethesda commuters have expressed their frustration while waiting to drive onto the installation this morning, as it appears that cocky little Master at Arms standing gate guard is really taking his sweet fucking time scrutinizing both sides of every goddamned ID handed to him.

"Get a load of Seaman 'Ray-Ban' over there, holding up IDs to match the face like we're at Threatcon Delta or some bullshit," said Chief Hospital Corpsman Lorenzo Cliff, as he waited ten cars back while watching that arrogant little E-nothing scour over common access cards (CAC) like some Jew-hating Gestapo demanding Gypsies show their papers.

"It's not as if those of us who actually work for a living have to be at muster on time, though, right?" Cliff added from the driver's seat of his 1992 Ford Festiva. "So I really don't mind just farting along here, hoping to cross the gate by lunchtime."

"I was going to give him the benefit of the doubt, but it looks like he doesn't even have one of those CAC scanners that takes extra time to process each ID," Marina Neuheisel, a Navy spouse who was concerned about not being one of the first customers to show up on time for the start of the Navy Exchange's summer clearance sale, said of the self-important little asshat.

"So, basically, fuck that guy," she added.

In addition to the inordinate amount of time the as-yet unidentified MA has spent poring over each and every CAC like it was the Rosetta-fucking-Stone, other commuters have been complaining about the manner in which the kid (who probably couldn't hack SEAL training and ended up the pathetic Navy cop he is now) has been rendering salutes to officers.

"I just love how he pops to full-on attention and slowly salutes every officer crossing the gate like he's standing goddamned honor guard duty at some war hero's funeral," said Yeoman 2nd Class Tyler McNeil, as he waited in line at the gate to receive his blessing to actually go to work and do his fucking job.

UPDATE: At press time, a majority of those who had made it onto base said their opinion of the kid standing gate guard had changed for the better after he checked their IDs and welcomed them onto the installation.

"I really appreciate the way he said 'Welcome to NSA Bethesda' as he handed back my ID," said one commuter. "He's just doing his job and keeping us safe."

BEHIND THE BLOG

This story had perhaps, the weirdest and funniest offline occurrence I've ever had.

When this article was first written, the author had some other base name. But when I was searching online for a good photo to accompany it, I found one from Bethesda, and decided to change the base to that.

Soon after it was published, I got a phone call. It was an agent with the Naval Criminal Investigative Service.

The call basically went like this:

Hello, this is Agent Smith with NCIS. Are you the owner of Duffel Blog?

I am.

I'm doing a follow-up on a story you published about the naval base in Bethesda. I need to know the real name of the author, since we think it's a sailor stationed here and he's giving away details about our security procedures.

I'm not giving you that information.

Well, look. We take base security seriously. We need to know his name.

I'm not giving you his name. I actually don't even know it to be honest. Let me do this. I'll contact the writer and ask him about it and then I'll email you back. Ok?

Ok.

…

I actually wasn't lying about not knowing the writer's identity. While most of the contributors trust me with their real names, "Ted Heller" never actually told me his and I never asked. All I had was his email address, so I sent him this right after I got off the phone: "Hey Ted, if you get this please call me."

He called me and I told him the story, and we of course laughed ourselves silly. Then we brainstormed how we would respond. I emailed the guy back:

"Just wanted to let you know that I corresponded with Ted Heller, and told him he was allegedly revealing top secret details about the Bethesda gate. He was appalled at the revelation.

Unfortunately, I don't know Heller's true identity. All I know is that I receive all of his article submissions via dead-drop right outside the NSA Bethesda commander's office at 1430 every Friday.

However, he has told me that he's ashamed over his OPSEC violation, and has agreed to voluntarily keel-haul himself. In one week, he is to go to an undisclosed location (I recommended Alaska), lash himself to a fishing trawler, and endure his punishment.

I hope this satisfies your request, and good luck with your investigation. Thank you for protecting the Bethesda base from such vile criminals.

Oh and of course, thank you for your service."

Military Absentee Ballots Delivered One Day Late, Would Have Swung Election For Romney

By Drew Ferrol

WASHINGTON – Sources confirmed today that hundreds of thousands of military absentee ballots were delivered hours after the deadline for them to be counted, with preliminary counts showing that they would have overturned the vote in several states and brought a victory for Gov. Mitt Romney.

Officials say the ballots were delivered late due to problems within the military mail system. Tracking invoices show the ballots sat in a warehouse for a month, then they were accidentally labeled as ammunition and shipped to Afghanistan. At Camp Dwyer, Marine Sgt. John Davis signed for them and was surprised at the contents.

"I told Gunny we got a bunch of ballots instead of ammo," Davis told investigators earlier today. "He told me to file a report of improper delivery and that the chain of command would take care of it. We didn't hear anything for three weeks. While we were waiting, we came under fire so we dumped a bunch of them in the Hescoes. We didn't dig those ones back out."

After military officials realized the initial error, the ballots were then sent back to the U.S. but suffered a series of setbacks.

Twelve boxes of ballots were dropped overboard during delivery to the *USS Kearsarge (LHD-3)* in the Persian Gulf, then while the ship sailed to Bahrain, postal clerks allegedly pocketed whatever ballots they wanted.

The remaining absentee ballots were loaded onto a C-130, but the flight was delayed until November 1st so the crew could get tax free pay for the month. Once the ballots arrived stateside they were promptly mailed to each state's counting facility, reaching their final destination on November 7th.

"It's a shame," Rear Adm. John Dawes said when asked for comment. "I expected a delay so I ordered that everyone cast their votes eight months ago. It's really unfortunate that our mail system failed us and directly affected the course of history."

Upon hearing the news, angry Republicans have begun a demand for a recount, but most military absentee voters have shrugged off the news, with many wondering whether the care packages their families sent six months ago were ever going to show up.

BEHIND THE BLOG

Long before the media was complaining about "fake news" impacting the outcome of the 2016 election, we were setting the trend.

Weeks before the 2012 presidential race between Mitt Romney and Barack Obama, we had this article lined up and ready to go. Like a news organization has pre-written obituaries, we had this for the day after the election, ready to change the name to whoever lost. In the case of 2012, that name was Mitt Romney.

As you would expect, the article blew up.

It was passed around like crazy on the right, and received tens of thousands of comments. Many of them were angry, and complaining about a stolen election. And amid all this, there were some brave commenters who waded in and tried to explain to the gullible that, no, this wasn't true. "It's a satire site."

To which I eventually got my favorite comment of all time: "Satire? What is that some sort of liberal code word?"

ISIS surrenders after reading veteran's open letter

By Joe Zieja

RAQQA, Syria — The leaders of ISIS collectively surrendered yesterday after reading a highly compelling open letter posted on the internet, according to an apologetic and heartfelt statement released by the terrorist group.

The open letter, written by former enlisted Army communications specialist Brian Murphy, was posted on his personal blog and shared to his 67 Twitter followers last week. The post went viral after Murphy spent most of his early separation pay on Twitter advertising.

In what is being called an "EPIC takedown" that "blasts" and "totally destroys" ISIS, Murphy starts with a long and detailed history of his military service, describing his experiences at basic training and his deployments to Afghanistan. He then presents a grammatically confusing exegesis of the Quran that simultaneously proves that neither he nor ISIS has ever read it.

"Ultimately," Murphy said, "the idea was to take the power and non-ego-threatening nature of a personal, private conversation and then make it even more powerful by removing the privacy. People are always sure to listen more intently and respond more rationally when they know they have a giant audience."

The ISIS reaction was widespread and unanimous: Terrorism is wrong, and nobody should do it.

"We've read literally thousands of highly researched, scholarly articles that deconstruct our view of Islam before," said Ahmed El-Masri, a reformed member of ISIS. "But there's just something about a letter that is so compelling, it's like he was talking right to me. And Mahmud, and Salim said the same thing — it was as though someone actually sent me a physical letter with papyrus from Paper Source, sealed it with that wax stuff, and put it in my mailbox."

"It was like all of a sudden I could understand his struggle," El-Masri said. "English is my second language, and I also confuse the many forms of 'there.' I could relate to a man with his own inner jihad. And now our jihad is over."

Bryan Murphy may have made his mark on history, but the usefulness of the open letter is far from over. As a result of the surrender, the US government has already begun other open letter campaigns to end racism, hunger, and using two spaces after a period.

'I Killed Osama Bin Laden': A 5.56mm Bullet Tells His Story

By Frederick Taub

WASHINGTON D.C. — Just days after former Navy SEAL Team 6 member Rob O'Neill kicked off an ugly row by saying that he killed Osama bin Laden, a single 5.56mm bullet has stepped forward to claim responsibility.

Sources confirmed the copper-jacketed lead NATO-compliant projectile — which hails from Lake City Army Ammunition Plant in northeastern Missouri — claims that both O'Neill's and former SEAL Matt Bissonnette's accounts of the raid on bin Laden's Abbottobad compound in 2011 are completely false.

"Bissonnette's a liar," the bullet explained in an exclusive interview with Fox News' Megyn Kelly. "Not only a liar but a damn liar. He and O'Neill didn't do a thing to kill that terrorist scum. Me entering that goat-lover's cranium at 900 meters a second did! And let me tell you, the human brain is a disgusting place."

The bullet also revealed that his announcement had spurred a criminal investigation by the Pentagon, which accuses him of disclosing classified ballistics.

"Things have worked out great though," the projectile said. "I've landed a great job with the Ferguson Police Department, a book deal, *and* a ghost writer. I'm set!"

The bullet further stated that his decision to speak out was prompted by the loss of his retirement benefits, which would have begun only three months after the fateful day in which he was fired at supersonic speed out of the barrel of an M-4 carbine.

"That dickhead O'Neill is actually complaining about how he lost his bennies retiring at 16 years when every retard Joe, Dick and Dimpus in the force knows you need to put in all 20 to get 100 percent," the bullet explained. "Look, I'm not going to blame everything on losing thousands of my friends in Afghanistan, but it certainly didn't help. You know what I say to O'Neill? You should try getting splattered into a cement wall at Mach 2.5 you neck-bearded attention whore!"

At press time, the 5.56mm bullet's claim to fame is already being disputed by the other 29 rounds it shared a magazine with and the M-4 carbine that fired it. Additionally, a visibly deformed .458 SOCOM is insisting that the 5.56 is nothing but a pogue FOB-guarding bitch round that actually spent the whole war chambered in a Ugandan's rifle at the Kandahar chow hall.

Duffel Blog correspondent G-Had contributed to this article.

For more from Duffel Blog, visit www.duffelblog.com.

You can also find us on Twitter and Instagram at @DuffelBlog, and on Facebook, at
www.facebook.com/duffelblog

Made in the USA
San Bernardino, CA
02 April 2017